SOMETHIN̶   J

Shravya Bhinder loves to find hidden stories around her and write novels about them. Formerly a corporate employee, she managed to flee the madness after a few years of boredom to become a full-time writer. She is a sucker for romance and strives to pen down exciting stories. When she is not reading and writing, she is out enjoying nature, playing with her dogs or cooking for her family.

    She lives in Melbourne with her family, in a house with a barren backyard and a lifetime's collection of books.

Something
I'm Waiting
To Tell
You

SHRAVYA BHINDER

EBURY
PRESS

An imprint of Penguin Random House

EBURY PRESS

USA | Canada | UK | Ireland | Australia
New Zealand | India | South Africa | China

Ebury Press is part of the Penguin Random House group of companies
whose addresses can be found at global.penguinrandomhouse.com

Published by Penguin Random House India Pvt. Ltd
4th Floor, Capital Tower 1, MG Road,
Gurugram 122 002, Haryana, India

Penguin
Random House
India

First published in Ebury Press by Penguin Random House India 2022

10 9 8 7 6 5 4 3 2

ISBN 9780143450245

Typeset in Bembo Std by MAP Systems, Bengaluru, India
Printed at Replika Press Pvt. Ltd, India

www.penguin.co.in

MIX
Paper from
responsible sources
FSC® C016779

Soulmate

I grew up watching a lot of Hindi movies. Bollywood conditions us to believe that our soulmate is the one who is a perfect fit for us. Most of us think that we are one half of a puzzle that the soulmate will complete when they walk into our lives. They will just fit and mould themselves to make us whole.

After having gone through many ups and downs in my life, I now know that Bollywood is wrong. We are not a puzzle, we are not incomplete beings, we are, in fact, complete in ourselves. We just do not know it yet. A soulmate is a person who shows us what we truly are, a person who challenges us to be the real us, a person who brings out the best in us not by becoming a part of us but by becoming a mirror to our soul. They help us lose our inhibitions, addictions, ego, and transform our lives just by being there. They need not mould us into someone else, they need not fit into the gaps that we feel within ourselves but they need to be able to shatter every obstacle around us so that we can grow fully. They open our hearts so that light can reach even the darkest places; they sometimes make us lose control only to awaken us.

A true soulmate is the only person we need, and a true soulmate is the only person we seldom meet . . .

*Whenever we meet new people, knowingly or unknowingly,
we become a part of their stories. Sometimes we leave these stories
midway and wonder what happened next.
When we exit a story, the story continues. The characters
continue to live their stories and explore their fate.
When* **you** *exited our story, we continued to live. Life happened
and so did many other things.
But before we get to our story, I have another story to tell you.
Another love story that needs to be told because that was where it
all began.
Let me take you to the year 1943.*

December 1943

To be able to go to London and study law was a dream, a dream that he never saw, a dream that was someone else's, and yet he was more than willing to fulfil it. It was his father's dream. Young Mohinder Kapoor was at war with himself; his heart told him to follow its lead while his head had its own plans. Mohinder's father wanted him to study law in London. He wanted Mohinder to make connections in the big city, which was the centre of the world for most people. The old man wanted only the best for his son and his business. He wished that one day Mohinder would be a man of influence, who would be more successful than the previous generations in the family; a man who could do as he pleased and not have to wait for others to decide his destiny. Senior Kapoor was not wrong as a father to wish the best for his child; he wanted a safe future for his son, a secure life that few people in the land could boast of.

What Mohinder wanted was not a question deemed important enough to be raised. Not that his father would have not let him fulfil his dreams, but it was never a question that was to be asked. In that day and age, it was assumed that all a son wanted to do was to continue the legacy of his family; all he should do was fulfil his parent's wishes. It was an unstated rule, and no one ever thought that a child could have their aspirations too. A girl child suffered more because she was initially supposed to fulfil the demands of her parents and get married as per their wishes. And then, she had to follow the rules of the new household and work on the wishes of the new family, which was mainly restricted to a male heir. Have the rules changed over the centuries? On the face of it, yes; but the essence remains the same. And, you know what? We mostly do what others expect us to—look happy on the outside while bit by bit our inner self breaks into millions of pieces trying to keep our loved ones happy.

Mohinder, too, wanted to fulfil the said duties of a son. He wished to be a painter and a writer, but he knew that, being the only son, it was his responsibility to take over his father's business of spices; to see that his family was well settled, financially. So he didn't utter a single word when his father decided his career path without any consultation as if he was not a part of it at all. He was a mere doer. But Mohinder was anticipating it; he knew that painting or writing was not a serious career choice if he had to earn well and provide for everyone around him, at least not in those times. And yet, when his baba told him to start packing for London to get his law degree, something inside him broke. He was to go away for years and not return even during breaks. At that time, travel was neither cheap nor convenient. While he had no qualms about getting on the life path decided by his family, his heart ached for his younger sister Radha's friend Raavi.

Raavi was their neighbour's daughter. Over the last few years, she had become a woman many dreamed of. Her out-of-control frizzy hair was now always shiny and fell around her face like a halo. Her skin looked illuminated in the sun and reflected the dim light of the moon. Her laughter always filled the room she was in and her perfume intoxicated Mohinder. She was everything that Mohinder was not—outspoken, witty, happy, charming and, most of all, she did what she wanted and not what she was told to do. Even though she loved her like her own daughter, Mohinder's mother called her a rebel and often jokingly warned Radha to steer clear of her. 'She will fall in love and run away, I tell you, and then you will miss her the most.' Radha just blinked rapidly, unable to decide on her reaction while Raavi stuck her tongue out and mocked the older woman. They were a family already and Mohinder marvelled at how good the entire set-up was. All he needed now was for Raavi to love him back, if not as much as he loved her, then just enough for her to agree to marry him. She was trouble and he wanted her to be his trouble.

While he knew that his mother loved the chatterbox who had frequented their home since they were kids, when and how he fell in love with Raavi was a mystery to him. All he knew was that he loved her; he loved her more than he had loved anyone before. He dreamt about being with her all his life. Initially, he had presumed that the recurrent thoughts about Raavi were the result of her constant presence in his house and life as his sister and Raavi had been inseparable since infancy. Then he started looking at her differently and noticed small things that he would have never seen otherwise. Like her smile—she had one crooked tooth that stood out as she smiled. It made her look so innocent and added to her charm. Her hair was darker than Radha's and longer, too. She moved her fingers a lot in her hair and tended to curl a few strands around her index finger when trying to explain something. She made a lot of funny faces when she was forced to drink milk and she cheated whenever they played a game of cards, unabashedly, with no care in the world!

But Mohinder never could muster the courage to talk to Raavi about how he felt, how his heart missed a beat every time he saw her dancing with his sister in the rain, or how he thought she would be the perfect daughter-in-law to his mother every time the duo fought and made up. He could not as, during those times, if you loved someone, courting or dating was out of the question. There was only one way of being with your beloved and that was through marriage. While he knew that the families would have been more than happy to be tied together for life through their alliance, that was not the right time as he didn't want his father to look at Raavi as a distraction in his son's life. Neither did he want to get married and then have to leave her in India and be in London all alone for two years, while she stayed far away, thinking about him. He knew that getting married and taking her along was out of the question as it would have been a very costly affair.

Even though he was very sure of his future with her, since his father declared that Mohinder was to go away for a few years, he wondered what would happen to his love. Till the day he was to leave, he kept contemplating whether he should confess his feelings. But contemplation without action leads nowhere. So, he went off, with all his love still in his heart and words echoing in his head. He stayed in London for three long years instead of two; every day hoping and praying that Raavi would not get engaged to marry anyone else. He wrote to Radha every week and she, too, corresponded regularly. The girls were now almost nineteen years old, and his sister was engaged to a young man in Delhi.

Finally, he came back after finishing law school. Radha was getting married that week and he promised his heart that as soon as she was off to her new home, he, too, would talk to his parents about getting married to Raavi. But first, he had to tell her how he felt and also ask her if she felt the same way. Living in London for the last few years, he knew how important it was for her to love him back if they were to live happily. He wanted her to like him enough and to find him suitable at the least before the families fixed it all. The families would have no issue with the alliance—that he was sure of.

So, he looked for her one evening and found her sitting alone, basking in the January sun on her terrace, which was joined on one side with theirs. She looked like a painting that he wished he had created. Her full lips, long lashes and dark hair made her look divine. Her eyes shaped like almonds were fixed on something in her hands as she faced the sun bravely and her skin looked golden. It was a beautiful sight to behold. A part of him didn't want to disturb her! All he wanted was to look at her for days. And that was all he did until he realized that someone was coming over to her, jumping several terraces—a man dressed in a black kurta-pajama. A man who was approaching Raavi with a smile plastered across his face, his eyes spoke of affection.

When he reached Raavi's terrace, Mohinder shouted at him, 'Oye! What do you want? Who are you?' His voice broke the peaceful state Raavi was in, enjoying the winter sun warming up her body.

She looked at the man and then at Mohinder wide-eyed. Her fingers touched her lips and with pleading eyes and shaking her head, she requested Mohinder not to scream. He was puzzled. As the man came nearer, she said, 'Please, for the love of God, do not say anything to anyone, Mohinder. We love each other.'

His world shattered in front of his eyes. But what else was he expecting? A girl as beautiful as her, as loveable as her, would remain hidden from the world? He was expecting a miracle when he had prayed that she'd be single when he returned. She was unmarried but in love with this man. He could see that in her eyes, the way her face lit up when he greeted her. She was in love with this man more than Mohinder was in love with her.

Later that evening when Raavi, Radha and Mohinder sat on the porch, she told him all about Raza, the goldsmith's son. He belonged to a rich Muslim family. However, she was worried that her parents would never agree to the match. 'His parents will not understand either. Even though our families are so close to each other, they won't get us married, you know . . .'

Mohinder felt a little happy with this information. There was a silver lining, after all! But then, the floor beneath him shook, when she added, 'But we plan to elope soon.'

'What? Are you mad?' he said suddenly, shrieking a bit. Radha punched him on his arm, 'Shush . . . *Dheere bolo* (speak softly),' she reminded her elder brother.

Radha was Raavi's confidante and she wanted her best friend to find her happiness even if it meant eloping with the man she loved and 'bringing shame to the family'—like her own mother had predicted she would do.

'You know that her father will have a second heart attack, don't you?' Mohinder reminded the young girls sitting in front of him.

They looked at each other with sad eyes for a moment and then Raavi said, 'Then you talk to them and make them understand. They love you so much, they can never say no to you.'

They loved him so much and could never say no to him . . . was the stupid reason why he had delayed the whole thing. It was why he never confessed his feelings, it was why he assumed that they would one day get married to each other, because her parents loved him so much and never said no to him!

Anyway, wounded and ready to get further scarred, he told Raavi that he would talk to her family after a few weeks. He needed time to align his thoughts and tame his heart. If he was to be the man that his parents had raised him to be, he had to be in the right frame of mind. So, Radha got married and moved to Delhi and every few days, Raavi reminded him of his promise.

It was in July 1947, when talks of Partition had begun. Mohinder and his family decided to move to Delhi to be close to Radha until all the hype had subsided. 'We will then come back and resume the business,' his father told his family. They planned to take only some possessions and, like most of their neighbours and friends, they too believed that it was a temporary move and things wouldn't change much. A few days before their journey, they dug a hole in their backyard and put all their cash there. 'Papa, we might not be able to come back. I have heard that we should carry our gold and property documents with us.' Mohinder had his sources and, if they were to be believed, this move would be permanent. Honestly, he didn't mind a permanent move. He wanted to be safe and any place close to his sister's house was a good move for the family. Raavi's family was also moving with them; they were all to take the same bus and then a train to Delhi.

His father decided to listen to his son, and they took all of their gold as well as documents along. The night they were boarding their bus, they had a visitor—Raza. Raavi and he began trying to convince his parents about their getting married. When they did not agree to the match, Raza decided to accompany Raavi's family to Delhi. 'I have my uncles there; we can get married and settle near Lucknow. They will help me get some work and I have some cash and jewellery to keep us going, if you allow,' Raza pleaded with Raavi's father. He was not happy; none of her family members were, but it was not the right time to argue. The boy was willing to leave his family and home for the sake of their daughter's love; they knew the boy and liked him too. Moreover, it was time to move and everything else had to wait.

So, all of them made the move. Raging with fury, Raza's brothers and father met them at the bus stand and warned of consequences that no one paid heed to. The news was that violence had broken out and it was safer to reach Delhi than to remain in the part of Punjab they were in. They, along with several others, boarded the bus.

After midnight, they reached the station and crammed into a train going to Delhi. Everyone was scared; the future was so uncertain suddenly. Looking around, the thought that they were moving permanently crept into everyone's mind. Mohinder's family was small—just him, his father and his mother. They found some space to be together. Raavi's parents, her three young brothers, one unmarried aunt and Raza couldn't fit in the same compartment.

'I will take care of them,' Mohinder said, as he held the hands of one of her three brothers and made the boys sit on the laps of the members of his family. Raavi's father just nodded and took the rest of his family to the next compartment.

Within minutes, they heard screams. When Mohinder looked out of the nearest window, he saw people running everywhere. Just outside the window stood Raza's elder brother, Mushtaq. He had a sword in his hand. And he was clutching someone's hair. Rage ran through Mohinder's body like an electric current when he realized that it was Raavi whom Mushtaq had forcefully pulled out of the train and was now holding at the point of his sword. Before he could react, do something, say something—Mushtaq dug his sword deep into her and her lifeless body dropped instantly. Tears filled Mohinder's eyes, and he heard a roar—it had come from his mouth. He was shivering, the realization hitting him that she was now dead.

All because she loved someone.

One by one, Mushtaq and his brothers killed Raavi's mother, father, aunt—even Raza. Mohinder froze where he was. No, he was not a coward. He wanted to kill them all with his bare hands and he knew that he could kill a few. He was a strong man, but they were armed and he was not. He also looked at the pale faces of Raavi's brothers who were so stunned that no words escaped their open mouths. His parents were crying, shocked at the horrific spectacle. They loved Raavi and her family, he loved Raavi and her family, but they were dead and all that remained were her three brothers. The train started moving slowly. People desperately wanted to cram into the train, so they stomped over the dead bodies. He couldn't bear the sight. Mohinder hugged the three kids in front of him. She was gone but he had to survive in order to give the ones who survived a life she deserved. His love for her was too strong. He had to do the right thing. She was gone but his love remained and, at that moment, he thought that it was all he needed to survive: his love for Raavi and his responsibilities towards the ones that mattered to him.

The rest of the journey was a blur. He could never recall anything that happened while they were on the train. The family reached Delhi and, unlike others who were taken to camps in and around Delhi, they were lucky to have his sister there. Along with the three boys, they went to her house. The scene in Delhi was worse than what he had witnessed in Punjab. In Radha's house, living with them was her friend, Naghma, whose family had been brutally killed a few nights ago. Partition had done unimaginable damage and so many lives had been destroyed over a matter of days.

Many, many months later, Mohinder found love again. He found love in Naghma. Pain brings people closer in ways one cannot imagine.

Naghma had lived through the same pain; her family of ten was brutally murdered when they were trying to board a train to Pakistan. Her relatives didn't keep her with them as she was a girl of marriageable age, a burden. She understood Mohinder's duty towards the three boys, and she was loved by his ageing parents for being selfless and loving. She understood Mohinder's pain. Her fiancé, who should have protected her, was now in Pakistan and hadn't bothered to come back looking for her.

In three years, Mohinder moved out of his sister's house. They were indebted to them for life but then, one should always be able to depend on one's family. And yet, people like Raza had lost their love, their lives at the hands of their own family—such was the irony!

Once they had settled in their new home, his mother suggested he get married. Mohinder could think of no one else but Naghma. She had slowly made her place in his heart. There was still love for Raavi; that would stay with him for life and maybe beyond, but now his heart had expanded to make space for Naghma. He told his mother the same thing.

'But she is a Muslim,' his mother said in a low voice.

'And?' Mohinder asked his mother to explain. He didn't expect her to object just because of her religion. 'We love her, we think she is perfect . . . it is just that her people killed Raavi,' his mother said with sorrowful eyes. 'We knew that you loved her, and her family had asked if, after coming to India, the two of you could get married,' she said, with tears rolling down her face.

She knew! All of them knew except Raavi! He felt a sudden pang in his heart. But Raavi was gone and it was no use hurting himself over her. Moreover, she had died loving someone else.

'But she loved someone else, Ma!' he said with a loud sigh. 'Naghma's people didn't kill Raavi. Our people did! They were our family friends, Raavi's family's friends . . . our neighbours. Naghma didn't even know them. If we go by that logic, then our people killed Naghma's family.'

His mother had no words; she hugged him to tell him that she was happy for him as long as he was sure. In a week they had two weddings, a Hindu temple wedding, and a nikaah.

Years later, when asked, Mohinder said that his love for Naghma made him brave enough to face new challenges.

She made him see himself as the person he was to become. She made him the best version of himself. Naghma, on the other hand, just said, 'Second chances! They are what we need to believe in, no matter what has happened in the past. Sometimes, you don't get it right the first time.'

But this book is not about Naghma and Mohinder. This book is about their great-granddaughter, Adira Kapoor.

This book is about second chances!

People wonder about life, our world, the world beyond our world.
I do not.

My world begins and ends with you.

Ronnie

I opened my eyes and blinked a few times. My vision was not exactly what could be termed 100 per cent clear but still, the sunlight bouncing off her silver charm bracelet caught my eye. It was in pieces just like my own heart; some charms were missing, the chain was broken into two pieces and the clasp that held the ends together was crushed.

In the light coming from a small opening in the curtains, the 'symbol of our undying love', as Adira used to refer to it ever so often, lay broken and rejected. It looked as if it had gone through enough during that night and needed no more unexpected twists and turns from life. It looked exactly like the person it belonged to—Adira looked the same to me. I moved my gaze over to the single bed. There she lay bruised but calm; unconscious but at peace. There lay the girl who deserved all the love and happiness in the world; my life, my love, my reason to smile, my motivation to be better than what I was yesterday, my reason to stop worrying about what had happened and think of the future.

It had been a few months since the accident and her body was still mostly unresponsive, but every time she opened her eyes, I knew that she remembered me, her mind knew who I was, and her heart remembered what I had done to her. The guilt was overwhelming.

I moved my chair closer to her bed. There was a scar on her forehead; her hair covered a part of it. I traced the mark with my fingers and felt guilt explode through my body. Her eyeballs were moving very slowly behind her closed eyelids as if she was dreaming of something serene and calm, like the sea or maybe music . . . she loves music. Her lips were parted slightly and she breathed softly, making hardly any sound. The rise and fall of her chest was calming to look at. The motion meant that she was alive, breathing, and recovering as I looked at her. I knew that she would one day get up and talk to me. I wondered what she remembered about me, about us. I took her hand in mine. Her delicate, skinny fingers lay limply in my big hands. Her index finger still had signs of the gold band that once was her constant companion. I curled my fingers and intertwined them in hers. Her hands were not as warm as I remembered them to be. I raised her fingers to my lips and kissed them lightly; her eyelids fluttered but she didn't open her eyes. I felt tears swelling in the corner of my eyes. The room smelt of medicines and floor cleaner and yet, as I moved my forehead to touch it with hers, I felt her fragrance fill me—British Rose. The smell was a lie; I knew it, but it gave me comfort to know that my mind remembered even the smallest of details.

Almost everyone who knew what had happened had told me that the accident was not my fault. Most believed that it was fate. She was at the wrong place at the wrong time. But I clearly remembered ignoring her pleas to head back home with me. I could still recall how rudely I had told her that she was 'dead to me'. Of course, I was not aware of what fate had in store for us next. It was true that no one could have predicted the accident when I let her go back with strangers. I was not aware of what could happen; probably it was in the destiny of that car to collide with the truck. But if I had behaved well with her, she would have not left in that car; if I would have been more considerate, we would have been together. If I would have not been the inconsiderate jerk that I was that evening, and mustered some courage to get down from the car to help the people stuck inside it after the accident, she would have been rescued from the wreck sooner. The others were dead upon impact, but she was alive and she had suffered for the next four hours before a passerby found her and took her to the hospital. How could I forgive myself for that? Maybe the accident was in her destiny, maybe it was to happen regardless of what had transpired between us that night. But what happened after that was my doing. I was there as she lay in the wreck, I was supposed to take her out, take her to the hospital, ensure that the blood loss was minimal. I was given a chance, I was given a way to be there for her when she needed me. But I was too drunk at that moment to think straight, to even walk straight for that matter. I failed her and I knew it. I had failed her on so many occasions and no matter what anyone else thought of my role in the entire scheme of things, I knew that I was the one to blame. I knew that I was wrong, I had wronged her!

I love her so much that if it were possible, I would go back in time and change everything that led to her being bedridden. If fate didn't permit that, then, at the very least, I would have taken her place. I would have happily taken all her suffering. But I could not because life does not always give you second chances at the same thing. I could not reverse time, I could never replace her. All I could do was to pray for her speedy recovery, help her in any and every way that I could, and hope that she would still love me when she regained her consciousness—if ever she did. The last bit was too much to ask for, and I knew that, but I was ready to work to get her love back.

I knew that it would be tough for her. She had been treated unfairly by not just me but also by fate, which she talked about so much. Every morning I tried to focus on the positives in life and not think of all the could-have-beens. I focused more on the amazing life we could build together when she got up and if she wanted to be with me. Honestly, I was somewhat looking forward to the day when she would get up to tell me how much she hated me, blame me for the time she had lost, despise me for the way I had treated her, get angry for the bruises my selfishness had given her. I was dying to hear her voice, see expressions on her face, the day she would recognize me again, cry again, get angry with me—do anything.

While my heart still clung to the idea of us falling in love again, I knew that was a lot to ask from her. I also knew that it was a lot of work for me to make her fall in love with me all over again, but I was looking forward to that too. After all, we never give up when things matter to us the most. When we give up on dreams, it means that we never really were very passionate about them, because with passion comes will, and with will comes the determination to reach our goals. Living a beautiful life with her was my goal, giving her everything that she deserved was my goal. And even if this time I would be unable to make her love me back, I would still be happy just knowing that she was happier away from me as long as she was healthy and loved her life the way it was.

For the last few days that I had been around her, I observed that now and then her eyelids fluttered. She had started blinking and moving her eyes. It was not a lot but was enough for all of us to believe that she was going to be well really soon.

Every time I visited her, her mother wanted me to go away. She did not like me anywhere near her daughter any more. She blamed me for her state and kept an eye on me the entire time I was around Adira. The only time I was alone with Adira was when she had a work call or was making food. She never really liked me; she had expressed her displeasure when Adira had told her about me and never thought that I was a match for her beautiful daughter. But since the accident, she'd come to hate me. I did not blame her. I also understand that she meant well; she meant well for her daughter who had trusted me. Had I been in her place, as a parent, I would have felt the same, done the same, and behaved in a worse manner. I would not have let the person responsible for my child's pain come anywhere near my child for life. Adira's mother was letting me come to visit her daughter. She even cooked me a meal when I stayed over. She doesn't blame me vocally; her silence says it all. My respect for the woman had been elevated to unimaginable heights because she is single-handedly taking care of Adira, her expenses, her care. I knew that I had messed up, I knew that I had taken her for granted, I knew that I had broken her heart and hurt her.

If I could go back in time and fix it, I would. I could not, though, no one could. I loved her, always did, and will always do. I prayed for her to get well every time I joined my hands to pray. I prayed for her to be able to listen to me when I repeatedly asked for her forgiveness sitting beside her. I prayed for her to forgive me, I prayed for her to take me back but mostly, I prayed for her to be herself again. For whether she gave me another chance or not, I prayed for her to live her life happily and in love, with me in it or without me.

I prayed for Adira to be well again.

You do not know what helplessness is until you go through it on your own. I would not wish for anyone to know the true meaning of helplessness. A lot is lost in trying to navigate between not understanding and truly understanding the meaning of this wretched word.

Adira

Chandigarh

'But I want to stay, please,' I heard a familiar voice. I knew that the voice belonged to someone I knew, someone I was close to, but who? I could not connect the voice to a face, or any voice to any face. My vision was blurry and I could not move my eyes, they felt as heavy as rocks. Yet this time when I came out of the darkness something felt different. With hope, I once again tried to move my limbs—nothing.

We hear of someone being helpless and think that we can understand what the state of helplessness is. It is a feeling when someone cannot help themselves, no matter how much they try—isn't it? The fact is, we never really understand the true meaning of helplessness until we are in the state. I was helpless as I recalled nothing, felt nothing, saw nothing. All I was capable of was hearing a few words every now and then; some clear, others incomprehensible. The words hardly made any sense to me without the context. Thankfully, I still knew who I was and the last memory of mine served enough to figure out why I was the way I was. I had been in a freak accident.

I could sense that there was definitely some light in the room— daytime, I deduced. Blurry movements happened right in front of me

22

and then came some whispers. There was more than one person in the room.

What was the day today?

Or even the date?

Some days, I wonder what happened to all the other people who were with me in the car that night. I hoped they had managed to escape but I could only wonder since I was not in a state to do anything else to satisfy my curiosity.

Pondering over what I recalled from my life, I felt the darkness return. My brain fogged.

The next time my blurry vision returned, the place was dark.

Night, I assumed. And then it happened.

Blink.

I felt my eyelids close and open. My surroundings remained dark but there was a definite flutter of my eyelids.

Is it possible to feel things that are not happening? I wondered.

I had been trying to feel something, anything, for so long that probably my mind was playing one of its nasty tricks—was my first thought. That explained it.

I wanted to drift back into sleep or whatever it was. The blurry visions and some sounds were the only impressions that had kept me feeling like a human being. I felt my breath going in and out of my lungs but was still unable to move. I heard a little groan in the room, someone was sleeping very close to me, and they groaned again—that was when it happened again.

Blink.

A few more blinks convinced me that it was indeed happening. I was blinking. The rest of my body was as non-responsive as it was the last time I checked. And suddenly my eyelids were once again as heavy as stones. The blinking stopped until I felt daylight hit my eyelids again.

Our brain is a funny little thing. It knows what is good for us and what is not—all good things are intensified and glorified in our memories and the bad ones are suppressed over time for them to hurt us less.

Adira

December 2019

What I felt during those months is now a blur. The world moved on without me, but I knew that there were only two people who did not. Only two people in the world whose lives froze in time in the hope that I would recover one day. It was probably this hope, their faith in me, their faith in destiny, that kept me alive, that made my body recover while the doctors had no clue why and how it was happening.

The accident broke three of my ribs, a leg, my shoulder was dislocated, but all this could be fixed. The doctors knew that. The body parts could be fixed. What they were not sure of were my brain, and my nervous system. I was in and out of a coma for some time. I lost my pulse on two different occasions and yet there I was, one and a half years later, sitting on the rooftop with my mother; listening to her, giving her weak smiles, which were all that she wanted. She was talking about an incident from my childhood that I do not have any memory of. Just like the accident that I do not remember much of.

She was telling me how I fell from a bicycle and then never really learnt how to ride. I could see her revisiting the scene; it was in her eyes. They sparkle every time she talks about my childhood. I love the sparkle in her eyes, it means the world to me now. My mother stood by my side, and nursed me back to health as if I was still a baby. This is how mothers are! Their love knows no bounds. No matter how old you are, they treat you like a child because you are their child. I will always be my mother's child. While I am physically almost well, my legs do give way at times and Mummy doesn't let me strain them. I still use a wheelchair, but hey, I am not complaining. I am alive and that is what is the most important thing. There is a slight limp in my walk and my left leg is weaker than the right one. The limp will stay for life as per the doctors and so will the scars under my ribcage unless I want to get them removed by surgery. But I do not, any scar or mark from any time in the past is important for me.

As time goes by, we tend to move on and start forgetting the things that made us who we are. It is these scars that remind us of everything that we have been through. Scars are precious, they are the time machines that transport us back to the past. My scars are most valuable to me; they remind me that I am alive even after going through something so intense. The scars remind me of my determination, my will to bounce back.

You will have guessed by now, one of the two people who believe in miracles and never gave up on me is my mother. And the second person will be here to visit me soon. He comes over every weekend, stays at a nearby hotel, and spends his days with me. Mummy doesn't like his presence in my life much. I do not blame her; she believes he is the reason why I couldn't feel anything for months, why I was like a vegetable and was bedridden. She wants him to leave as soon as he arrives, but she doesn't say much. They greet each other and she leaves me in his company. They do not talk but I can see in her eyes that she doesn't like him enough even to be cordial with him.

But I do, I still do. Sometimes your feelings are beyond your control, beyond the notion of right or wrong, beyond everything that logic dictates. Even after what happened I still wait for the weekends. I ask my mother to pick out my best clothes. She always says that I look amazing to her in my PJs, which I wear most of the time as they are the most comfortable, but I want to make an effort for him because he makes an effort for me. Every Friday after work he takes a bus from Delhi to Chandigarh to be with me over the weekend. He makes an effort to bring Samba along as I love to meet him. He plans the weekend and gets an old Hindi movie along for us to watch together. He updates a new playlist on my iPod every time he leaves—old Hindi classics because they are my favourite. While away on weekdays, he still drops in a text as soon as he wakes up and calls me each time he boards the metro—but we do not talk much. Because we can't. There are several reasons why—I still have slurred speech and am undergoing therapy. I do not like hurting my mother as she doesn't want me to get back on the same path that nearly led me to my own destruction. My mother had been with me like a rock while I was at my lowest and she didn't want me to be with Ronnie for my own good. Also, because there was not much left to talk about.

I wonder if love can die. Can it? Or maybe I had just fallen out of love because he fell out of love first and now he had fallen in love again, but all I have in my heart for him is respect because he never left my side.

Sometimes I wonder if I am going crazy. I mean, I would consider it to be a possibility as sometimes I daydream and these dreams are not just very real dreams—the ones you wake up from sweating in your bed and shaking all over—these dreams are much more than that. These dreams are like reality; mostly my eyes are open, and I am transported into the past, never to the accident but to the events that occurred around it. I see things happening right in front of my eyes, I feel them happening to me, I feel touches, pain, heat, breeze; everything. My mind at times is not able to differentiate between these dreams and reality. I have, over the months, however, learned how to differentiate and I mostly can by pinching or biting myself hard. If it hurts, it is real; if it doesn't, it isn't. But sometimes even that doesn't work. I am worried that my hallucinations are impacting my mother too, she looks scared every time I jolt out of these daydreams. She loves me, I love her back, he loves me too, but I wonder if I will be able to fall in love with him again.

Love needs to be taken care of. Love gets stronger when it is nurtured with more love, every day.
Love thrives on love.

Adira

Love is what makes the world go around. Love is what keeps everyone going. It can be your love for a parent, child, sibling, friend, lover, or a dream. But love is the basis of life. That is what I used to think. That is what I kept telling myself every time I felt love going away from me.

The thought that one could fall out of love never occurred to me until the day my mother mentioned it. My father and mother were getting a divorce. When I asked them why, my father just said that he loved me and would be there for me no matter what. His love for me would never lessen. My mother on the other hand remained quiet. She said that she would let me know one day when she got the answer herself. I was young and was honestly falling in love with a boy I had known for years—Raunak.

I understood love, the feeling that makes you burn when that person is close to you. A feeling that makes you giddy and stupid; that makes you believe everything is possible. I was experiencing the initial phase of love and was over the moon but, looking at my parents, I wondered if our fate would be

the same. I had not confessed my love for him. My parents'
separation had kept me busy and worried, to say the least.

And then one day my mother told me the reason why she
and Dad couldn't stay together any longer. 'We fell out of love,'
she simply stated.

'Is that possible? Why did you fall out of love and when?'
I asked her, unable to understand how and why anyone could
fall out of love!

'When you love someone, you think that nothing they do
will ever hurt you enough to unlove them, nothing that they
say can make you not want them, nothing can make you fall
out of love, for love is for life, isn't it?' my mother said lovingly,
as she patted my back.

I nodded and she carried on, 'Sometimes it takes a moment
to fall out of love and sometimes years. Your dad and I, over
many years, became different individuals as compared to the
ones we were when we got married. Our priorities changed,
our outlook towards life, needs, aspirations, everything that
was so aligned years ago, now are completely different. As we
evolved into these two people, we grew separately and we also
grew apart. We fell out of love without realizing that we were.'
She had tears in the corners of her eyes.

'When did you know?' I asked her in a low voice, moving
closer to her. I hugged her like I always did when I felt sad.
I was sad for her and I was scared for myself. *Did this happen to
everyone? Does everyone fall out of love?*

'I don't know. I realized it when your father said it out loud
but somewhere I knew it. I just do not remember since when.'
She was not blaming Dad for the divorce, and I knew it, but
listening to her tell me that Dad was the one who initiated it

made me take sides. I sided with my mother. It is a very natural thing to take the side of one parent, the one you think is right, the one you think has been wronged, the one you love more. Even though it was a mutual decision to part and my mother explained it in as many words, I still took her side because I loved her more.

That conversation made me doubt my love, my feelings, his love, his sincerity, the fact that we could also grow into two different people, complete opposites who would want different things in life—then what? A separation after years or maybe months . . . who knows!

This made me keep my feelings to myself, while he pursued me, wooed me for months.

But time makes you forget everything, and it did so. Finally, I said 'Yes' to him and confessed my feelings. It was tough for me but I had seen my best friend get married and it kind of made me believe in love once again. 'Probably what happened with my parents happens occasionally,' I reasoned in my head and life was blissful.

Ronnie and I were in love, he loved me beyond words and nothing could make us fall out of love. So we moved in together.

That's when I started noticing small changes. I called my mother worriedly after a few days, 'Mummy, do you think there was anything that you and Dad could have done to not have fallen out of love? To have grown together instead of individually?'

'Is everything okay between the two of you?' she asked.

'Yes! I just wanted to know, you know,' I lied and prayed that she would not ask any more questions. Tears were welling in my eyes, ready to fall.

'Hmmm . . . I . . . I don't . . . well, to think of it . . . we . . .'
She was trying hard to explain it to me knowing very well that
I needed her advice.

'Adira, I think if two people can work on it together, give
each other time, talk out the differences, then I guess it will be
possible to stay in love forever. This is what everyone told us to
do, this is what we eventually tried but it was too late by then.
I think the moment one sees a small crack in a relationship
and if one truly cares about it, the repair work should begin.
Words, communication, and the will to understand the other
person's opinion heal the open wounds in a relationship. The
sooner one begins the better.' She sounded sure of what she
was saying, and this was the first relationship advice anyone had
given me in a long time.

'I mean, if your dad and I would have realized that we
needed to do our bit to keep our love alive, to keep 'us' going,
we would have started talking initially. But as I said, we were
late and that is why our love succumbed.'

So, as soon as the phone call ended, I knew what I had to
do, I had to try and Ronnie had to try, too. But before I could
ask him to do his bit, I had to begin with mine. So, I started
talking to him, giving him his space, trying to resolve and not
argue. Did it work? Not in my case!

But I was stubborn and kept trying and trying. It took a
freak accident for me to realize that our love was not for life.
I nearly lost my life in the process and lost my ability to move,
see, talk and unconditionally love any other being.

For years the romance novels on my bookshelf had told
me that love was the Force, love was the most important thing,
love could never die, love prevails, it is not possible to fall out
of love with the person who has your heart.

Did I still believe in what I had read? Could I still be in love with him?

Simply put, I had fallen out of love. I realized after the accident that it was indeed possible to fall out of love. It may happen all of a sudden in a moment or over many years, but it can happen. It happened with me over several months but it took me a moment to realize it. As I was leaving the party that night, I heard the newly-weds Piyush and Tamanna—my idea of a perfect couple—fighting in the bathroom. I heard Tamanna scream about how much she regretted getting married. Piyush said, 'Love died.' This was the moment that made me realize that I too had fallen out of love, and so had Ronnie. We had become each other's comfort zones, someone to come back home to. There was no feeling of love but just a sense of familiarity that kept us together.

I decided that I had had enough of him ignoring me, I had had enough of being sidelined for something more important. I decided to take charge. Little did I know that the moment I decided to write my destiny, destiny wrote my fate in black ink.

Sadly for me, when I finally did resolve to get out of a relationship with an emotionally unavailable person, life threw me a bouncer and hit me hard. I got into a car with some other people, they were chatty and drunk and I was planning my next move—I had to gather all my things and move out. I wondered, where could I go? Tamanna would have been more than happy to help me but I now knew well that she was probably more stuck than I was—she was married to a man she didn't love.

'Mummy was right,' I said absent-mindedly and had to apologize as the woman next to me stopped her conversation and looked at me with worried eyes. *Did the aura of despair emit*

from me so much? Was I looking like the mess I felt I was? Maybe
or maybe not. I didn't have much time to ponder. My mind
was made up, I had decided to go back and live with Mummy
for some time as I needed her. I needed to be with my mother,
talk to her and feel at home, she was the only home I knew
of. I was her child and will always be but, until that moment,
I didn't realize how much I depended upon my mother for
emotional support and guidance.

I fiddled with my bag and found my phone. I had to check
if there was a flight or a bus available in the next few hours.
Before I could unlock the screen, my body was being flung
out of the car. I remember looking at the panicked faces of my
friends. No one in the backseat was wearing a seat belt; this is
the norm in India. Glass shattered, I felt something heavy land
on me; it was a person. I was crushed awkwardly under his or
her weight. There was one more jolt and then everything went
dark. These were my last memories and I know nothing of
what happened next.

Trepidation—a feeling of fear or anxiety that something is about to happen.

Ronnie

24 March 2020
New Delhi

I was working from home that day and work-from-home mornings were usually rather lazy for me. My life was settled in my new routine. My weekends were spent with Adira in Chandigarh. Monday was my usual workday; my parents had gone back to the UK to help my sister with her baby number two on the way. It was a girl, and my mother was thrilled beyond words. I spoke to my parents every day when it was convenient for them. Tuesday was a work-from-home set-up for me as I used to spend the afternoon with Nani. Since my parents were out of the country, I made it a point to spend a day with her and keep her company. Wednesday, Thursday and Friday were usual workdays with a few visits to my cousins who were now all married. Piyush and Tamanna had had a baby some months ago and were mostly busy. I was the babysitter they always needed and never paid. But I was happy with the set-up. After Adira's accident, I remembered to keep all my loved ones close to me and make time for the ones who mattered the most. After all, our relations are all that we have—jobs, money, success, etc. are all secondary and I finally had got my priorities right. I also had another thing that I was working on; it was my idea that would make the world a better place. I had been working on it after work every day.

But my world shook as I heard the news; India was going into a lockdown for twenty-one days due to the pandemic. I had my Nani to look after in Delhi, my parents were stuck in the UK, unable to fly back even if they wanted to. I couldn't visit Adira for three weeks and a deadly virus was taking over the country as I counted my miseries. Frantically, I called Piyush. Tamanna and Piyush had traveled to her Bengaluru home and were to come back on Friday. Unfortunately, they had to cancel their flight and now were to stay in Bengaluru for the next three weeks. It was a state of havoc and no one knew what to expect. Fortunately, Nani's in-house nurse called in to say that she would be willing to stay over and help Nani during the lockdown and I was so thankful for her generosity.

I made a quick visit to Nani's house, got a list of things needed for the next three weeks, picked up Samba as it was better if the cuddle bomb stayed at my house and not pester the nurse with all his unreasonable demands and needs. With the lists I headed over to the nearby shops. The scene at the market was something I can never forget. It was chaotic at best. People were shoving each other, bad-mouthing the authorities, cursing shopkeepers. Even though everyone had a mask on their faces, most people were wearing theirs under their mouths, protecting their chins from a zit of some sort. The prices of groceries were much higher than the MRP.

'This is not how we are supposed to wear a mask,' I politely told the person standing in front of me in the queue at the large convenience store.

'I am asthmatic, I can die,' she said, looking up at me.

'You cannot die because of a mask,' I stated as a matter of fact, realizing a little too late that most of the people around me were on her side.

'You know everything, don't you?' an elderly man said. 'He is a doctor,' someone else chimed in. 'You take care of your mask, do not worry about others, okay?' came another voice. That was the moment I learned a vital lesson: Corona or no corona, I should stick to my responsibilities as people do not want to be schooled by a random stranger.

Because of the panic, the sudden news of the lockdown had spread. No one cared about the prices as long as the things they wanted to hoard were available. It took me five hours to complete the runs and still many items, including many of Nani's medicines, were not available.

Trepidation was all that one could sense across the city.

A few months ago, Nani had been diagnosed with breast cancer. She was at the advanced stage; she was undergoing chemo and was fragile. Mummy and my other *masi* (maternal aunt) were her constant companions and took care of all her needs. But then Mummy went to the UK and Masi had to take all the responsibility on her shoulders. With Piyush's new baby and the endless fatherly responsibilities that came with her, things got a bit more exhausting, and we got an in-house nurse so that Nani could get the support she needed. While the nurse stayed in the house all day, some family member or the other stayed over at night. I was worried and called Nani's doctor to check what would happen to Nani's chemo session in the coming week.

'Corona is deadly for people with underlying conditions so I would advise we wait it out,' the doctor told me. I was also advised to inform all the relatives not to visit as Nani could catch the virus and it could harm her the most because of our carelessness.

Calling everyone, reminding them not to visit Nani, checking if anyone needed me to help them in any way took me another few hours. At nine in the night, I dropped in a text to Adira: AWAKE?

YES came her reply instantly.

CAN WE TALK? I asked. She talked less over the phone mainly due to her mother and partially due to the slur in her speech. While there had been a major improvement in her speech as well as her walk over the recent months, she was still very conscious of the changes.

I AM IN BED ALREADY, WE CAN CHAT she texted and I didn't put any pressure on her to call me instead. I was happy with whatever she wanted as long as she let me be a part of her life. We were not together any more but she was always concerned about my life, health, job . . . everything.

SURE I texted her and then checked if she knew about the coronavirus and the lockdown.

Though she had no underlying conditions, her body was still weak and recovering. I didn't want her to take any chances. She knew about the lockdown and her mother had prepared the house for the worst situation. Mrs Kapoor is a true hoarder and very resourceful. This was a reason I could sleep peacefully at night; her mother knew how to get things done. She was much better at managing people and tasks than most men that I knew. She was a strong woman and Adira had inherited her traits. I dropped a short message to her mother asking her if she needed me for anything. She didn't respond but I had made myself available and she knew that she could depend on me. Whether she liked it or not, I was always there for her and her daughter.

Not taking up a lot of her nap time, I said goodnight to Adira and she went off to sleep. I, on the other hand, scrolled through her pictures on my phone. They had been taken recently; her mother had hired a photographer when Adira had taken her first few steps. In one of the pictures, dressed in a blue maxi dress, she was standing next to a tree in their neighbourhood park. Her eyes sparkled like those of a child when they learn how to walk. Her mother was with her in most of the pictures. Her beautiful smile reaching her eyes was mesmerizing. The mother and daughter looked so much alike! One could also see the glow of pride on their faces—they had come a long way. Adira had come a long way. In the picture, she looked like the sun, beautiful and bright—blinding even. She had always been my sun and I, like a lost planet, looked up to her, waiting for her to rise—my life revolved around her. My existence, my ecosystem, everything depended upon her.

Looking at her beautiful pictures, with Samba snoring loudly under my bed, I revisited our happy memories and drifted off to sleep.

I am not alone in this journey. You are my constant companion, though you might not know it, a part of your heart is always beating in my body.

Adira

A lockdown was going on. Mummy was coordinating with her vendors and clients over the phone. After my parents' separation, Mummy used her contacts to start a party-planning business. It was nothing big, compared to the companies they show in the movies, but Mummy loved being independent. She was sitting in the living area, talking animatedly and sometimes borderline yelling at her staff. I couldn't help but smile. I directed my wheelchair towards her. Though I could walk on my own, in the mornings, I liked to take it a little slow. I was still not very confident about walking alone or without support. My physiotherapist came in thrice a week and I loved spending time with her. She was almost my age and she and I had become friends. We chatted about almost everything under the sun for the entire two hours that she made me exercise. She was due to come over the day the lockdown was announced, but sent me a text the previous night, cancelling her appointment. I didn't expect her during the lockdown; physiotherapy was not an essential service but her presence in my life was, so I was a little disappointed to know that she would not meet me for at least three weeks.

Her name is Samantha, I called her 'Sam', the way she prefers it. I was inspired by how independent she was, just like my mother. Looking at these two women, I too wanted to do something someday, something to be proud of, but I was yet to determine what that 'something' was. Sam had begged me to continue with my exercises and I hoped Mummy would not mind taking me to the terrace as I hated working out indoors. I liked it when the rays of the sun hit my skin and made me feel alive. I liked the breeze in my hair and the sounds of life buzzing around me. We had a number of stray dogs in the neighbourhood and they made a lot of noise during odd hours; every passing car, scooter, or person was given due attention. While the heat, noise and chaos were bothersome for many, they made me feel alive. These things made my life bright and I needed this brightness to colour my life.

As I approached the sofa in the living room, my mother's focus shifted from her own call with her 'lazy' worker to me. They were both wearing masks and my mother signalled towards the centre table, where there was a packet of blue and white disposable masks. I quickly obeyed and though I could not see her mouth, from her eyes I could tell that she was giving me one of her signature smiles. I smiled back and waited for her to say her goodbyes to the person in front of her and then to the people on the call.

'These lazy workers, I tell you,' Mummy said, releasing a breath as soon as the call ended. She took a dollop of hand sanitizer and rubbed her palms together. Though I had not even said hello to the visitor, she extended her hand for me to do the same. I placed my palm underneath the pump and was rewarded with sanitizer.

'You work too hard at times', I wanted to tell my mother and then it hit me: it was the wrong way to look at things.

My mother is the way she is because she has to be; she had no other choice. Her life had not been fair and she had learnt things the hard way. She was there for me when I needed her and could help me because of the way she was. I would not want her to change. I loved her exactly the way she was!

'Sam is not coming over; she wants me to continue with my exercises. Will you help me, Ma?'

'Of course I will help! I have done these calls early because I know that we will have more on our plate today. I was not expecting this man, but some people have no regard for instructions even when they come down from the ministry or the government.' She was referring to the man who'd left our house a few moments ago and I wondered if he was one of the few people who had disregarded the lockdown. 'The maid won't come either and neither will the cook.' With a full-time working mother, we were so used to all the house help that their presence was taken for granted. Taking care of ourselves and the house was going to be an experience!

'It is so quiet in here with no one around,' I told her as she wheeled my chair into the study.

'Where do you want to do your exercises?' Mummy asked me as she placed her journals and notebooks neatly on the racks. My mother has always been the one who would shoulder responsibilities and not even once think that it was all getting too much. She always had a lot on her plate and hardly ever took a break. With the new pandemic-induced changes, I was beginning to get worried for her. I wanted her to take a break.

'I was hoping we could go to the terrace. It is a warm day and I could do with some sunshine.'

I was expecting some resistance as she was always neck-deep in work but, to my surprise, Mummy agreed instantly and helped me out of the wheelchair. I could now climb the stairs too, but the limp didn't exactly make it easy. So, Mummy held my right hand while I held on to the railing with my left. One step after another, and together we reached our destination slowly and steadily.

'The limp will go soon,' Mummy said, as if she could read my mind. I was wondering if it would ever go. Doctors said it would be there for life but the same doctors also said I would never wake up. Sometimes doctors can be wrong, too, sometimes they miscalculate, and sometimes, God is very kind.

There was an outdoor bed, two chairs and a table on our terrace. The furniture was fairly new as I liked spending time there and Mummy wanted me to sit and not overwork myself as I practised walking and took my physiotherapy sessions. Also, there was an old gazebo to shield us when the sun got very harsh. I found it on OLX some weeks ago at a decent price. As the days became warmer, the gazebo was much needed.

That was a pleasant morning. It was a little past nine and birds still chirped around. Mummy is an early riser and I have fallen into the same habit. Before we began my exercises, we stood still and looked around; it was serene and beautiful.

I had a set of three exercises and I was supposed to repeat it three times. However, after two sets, I gave up and so did my mother. Her face turned red and her huffs and puffs were unmissable. 'Thank you, Ma, that is enough for the day,' I told her, putting her out of her misery.

'We can manage one more set, I think. I am not that old yet.' She squinted as the sun was blinding her and she needed water.

'It is more than I can manage, Ma. You are not old but I am still broken,' I told her, pouting.

She tapped me on my shoulder, 'Nah! You are fine and you will be better soon.'

Mummy headed downstairs to get us some water and I shouted after her, 'Get my earplugs, please.'

Mummy had to get back to work and I did not wish to go anywhere but to the sunbed to enjoy some more sun. 'I shall come back in one hour to check on you. Try and walk a little,' Mummy instructed before leaving a green water bottle and my earplugs beside me and turning on her heel to go back to her work.

I connected my EarPods and went to my phone's music; old Hindi songs were what I was after. My playlist has always been simple—Rafi, Kishore Kumar, Lata Mangeshkar . . .

After ten minutes of sunning, I started walking and then swaying a little to the music—this was my little paradise. After around three minutes, but what felt like half an hour or more to my legs, I sat down on the yellow sunbed panting like I had run a marathon. I closed my eyes and tried to calm my breathing when I heard something over my head and my eyes snapped open. It was a drone buzzing over. Honestly, it scared the crap out of me.

I squealed and moved back on the sunbed, not taking my eyes off it for very long and, at the same time, frantically looking around to see where it had come from. Much to my surprise, the machine dropped to the ground after a while. I didn't know how these things operated and wondered if it was a stray; like a bird or something that had lost its way and now was out of battery or something. I kept staring at it with my head tilted to one side, something that I noticed a few seconds later and aligned my head properly.

I had never seen a drone up close till then, so naturally, I was a bit inquisitive. I picked it up; it was not feather-light but was not very heavy either. There was a note attached to the base, which just read:

'You dance very well.'

Under normal circumstances, the note would have scared me. There was someone out there watching me as I danced, thinking that I was dancing without an audience. That was creepy. But this person had reached out to tell me that they were there, watching, and it made it a tad less creepy. Also, after everything that I had gone through, most people that I had met were my family and friends and they knew what had happened; they pitied me. I always felt that they were comparing my present life with my past and that thought was not a comforting one. I constantly felt the need for a new friend, someone who didn't know me before and saw me as I was with no comparisons. Though this was not the ideal way to meet a new friend, I knew that it was not bad either.

I looked around squinting my eyes to try and spot the person behind the machine and there he was. Yes, 'he'. I had not expected my admirer to be a girl and so I was not taken aback when he waved at me. He was standing on a terrace three houses away from the one right across ours. The sun shone brightly right above him. It was not very easy to see what he looked like but I did manage to see that he had a very welcoming smile and looked to be in his late twenties. He was wearing rimmed spectacles and a formal shirt as if he was working on the terrace. Maybe he was working from home like everyone else was that day.

I turned to see if I had something to scribble with, but who keeps a pen on their terrace? Exactly! No one and we didn't have one either. So I just bowed theatrically and accepted his compliment. I couldn't help but control my smile and he laughed heartily. That was exactly the moment when his drone buzzed and I let it fly back to him. He attached another note and sent it to me; it had his number and name. His name was Siddharth Sharma and he wanted to be friends with me. I did too, for my best friend was now a mommy and my mommy was now my best friend. I needed some new people in my life. I quickly picked up my phone from my table and dialed his number. It was funny really, to be talking to someone over the phone when otherwise, you could just open the door and walk up to them, if there wasn't a lockdown.

'Thanks for the compliment,' I said as soon as he picked up and heard his hearty laugh.

'So, for how long have you been stalking me?' I asked, looking at him and seeing him squirm. He was not very good at hiding his emotions and he reminded me of Ronnie.

'I . . . I actually . . . saw you yesterday with your mother,' he said.

'How do you know that it was my mother?' I placed my index finger on my chin. He ran his fingers through his hair.

'My mother told me. She knows your mum, okay? I was not being a creep or maybe I was. Sorry. But I like the way you dance and wanted to know you . . .'

'Are you Sharma Aunty's son?' I interrupted him by figuring out the puzzle. He was for sure Mrs Sharma's son who worked in Delhi, the one that Aunty keeps complaining about, the one who hardly comes over to be with his parents because he has so much work to do. The son who took them from rags to riches within a few years with his hard work and the one that she is very proud of. Sharma Aunty is my mother's friend and kitty partner. While a lot of food is exchanged between the two households and I love when Sharma Aunty sends over her famous kadhi rice, I had never bothered to look at her son's pictures in her house. It was neither appropriate nor necessary. I assumed that he would be someone older and definitely more pensive-looking. But looking at Sid, I could say that he'd chosen his DNA well. He was tall, much taller than my five-foot-five frame, broad as if he worked out often, and had a stubble which could have been the result of too much work-from-home but suited his face well. I was still amazed that Sharma Aunty had not told Mummy about her son's much-awaited arrival. Mostly, both Aunty and her husband visited Siddharth in Delhi as he was immersed in his work even during weekends.

'Yes, I am. So you know my mother?' he asked, as if I was the one who had been looking at him from afar for the last two days.

'We do. In fact, she is my mother's friend and I do not think that either of our mothers would like you snooping around like this.' I knew I was taking it too far so I giggled. He combed his hair with his fingers again. Maybe this was his giveaway, his way to hide his discomfort.

'My mother would like that I am finally talking to someone she knows. She wants me to go out and meet people,' he said bashfully.

'Good for you. I got to go. See you later then!' I said and waved at him.

He didn't wave back, just smiled and nodded once. I headed back downstairs to leave him with his drone and to tell Mummy what happened. I did feel his eyes following me. He was definitely a nice guy going by what his mother had told us but I was not looking for anything more than friendship and, in my heart, I was very clear about it. I didn't want him to get any ideas and I didn't want to lose control of my heart either. As I bolted the door of the terrace, I heard his drone fly back to him. I paused at the last step and saved his number with his name.

Mummy was still busy on the phone when I went into her home office and I sat down quietly on the two-seater couch in front of the window. She worked way too hard for her age, and I so wanted to help her but she never let me and that hurt me the most. I had started making plans of getting back to some work as soon as my doctor cleared me. It would have happened sooner had the Covid disaster not struck the world but I knew better than to complain. It was a miracle of sorts that I was alive and breathing and that was enough for my mother. I planned to take up some work from her so that she could find some time for herself and I, too, would get a sense of purpose.

It was around noon that Mummy got free from her work and I told her all about my interaction with Siddharth that morning. She was as shocked as I was that Sharma Aunty had kept her son's homecoming a secret. After lunch, Mummy called Aunty to confront her and later the phone call became a gossip session for the two ladies. I picked up a self-help book from Mummy's reading nook and busied myself for the remainder of the afternoon.

Mummy called me for dinner, and I neatly folded and placed a tissue lying on the table as a bookmark. It is an old habit. No matter how many fancy bookmarks I get, I always end up using the weirdest things to mark the last page I have read. Sometimes, it can be as bad as the wire of my phone's charger.

While our dinner was quiet and relaxed, I was itching to go back to my room and finish reading the book. I was at a very delicate moment in the book and needed to get lost in a place that promised security. The book I was reading gave me just that.

At the table, Mummy told me how she thinks that Sid and I should be talking more and once the lockdown was over maybe even go out for a movie or something. I knew what she was hinting at. I was no fool and the hostility between Ronnie and Mummy was not a mystery. They liked each other as much as Coyote liked the Roadrunner but Mummy was the Coyote, and always trying to hurt the poor Roadrunner. I didn't want an argument around Ronnie or Sid—men were the least of my problems at that moment and I was happy to concentrate on myself. So I just nodded and that satisfied my mother. She picked up her plate and moved on from the subject.

'Eat well, the doctor said you will need as much strength as you can get,' Mummy scolded me in her usual caring tone and I smiled at her. She thought of me and cared for me as if I was still a child who could not take care of herself. That was true only partially. I could now take care of myself; I just didn't think that I needed to while Mummy was around. I stuffed myself with rajma chawal and kissed Mummy goodnight. She planned to surf Netflix and Prime Video most of the night for a movie to watch, eventually watching nothing or a rerun of her favourite series and then complaining the next day about the lack of content nowadays.

As much as I wanted to step into the warmth of my book, the flickering light on my phone kept me from it. It was a video call. I picked up my phone and sighed. It was Ronnie. I knew he was calling to check if I was okay. It was his customary call, every evening. Post his parents' move to the UK, he had been taking care of his Nani and I was impressed with the way he was managing everything. I knew that his Nani had been diagnosed with cancer and that he was the one taking her to the chemo sessions, but he didn't even tell me. He didn't want me to get upset over Nani's health I guess, but Tamanna told me, unaware of Ronnie's intentions. I looked forward to his customary calls and texts—they meant that everything with him and his family was fine. Even though I was not sure of how I felt, I knew that I cared for him deeply and I also cared for Tamanna and Piyush who'd became parents recently. They had named their daughter Adira and I adore her. I couldn't help but smile at the thought of Adira, she was the cutest little thing in the world and I couldn't wait to hold her. Closing the door of my room, I answered the video call. Ronnie's face filled my phone's screen.

'Hey,' Ronnie said as soon as the call connected. I could see that he was perched on his sofa. It is funny the way I still remembered the minute details of his home. I had believed that it was my future home too. We were so happy, so much in love then. I massaged my aching legs and smiled back at him. His eyes twinkled every time we got on a video call and honestly, it is this twinkle that takes me back in time.

'How is the lockdown treating you?' I asked, trying to sound chirpy as I pressed my heels. They hurt like hell at the end of the day.

'I just finished some work and took care of Nani. She has caught a stomach bug. How was your day?' He was always keener to make me talk.

'Nothing major, I was free as usual. No work for me!' I laughed a fake laugh, but he could see through me. He knew that I wanted to get back to the work life soon.

'Work will happen in its due course. You should just take care of your health and relax.'

'I know. I am relaxing as much as I can. How is Tamanna? She called me and I missed it. When I called her back, she didn't pick up . . . must have been busy,' I said.

Even though Tamanna and Piyush fought all the time, I knew now that they loved each other. Their fights are their way of telling each other how much they care. *If only I had known it then* . . .

'They are good. I spoke to Piyush a few hours ago. They are super busy with Adira. Wooow . . .' this was when Samba jumped on him to say hello to me.

'Hey baby, how are you?' I asked Samba and saw Ronnie's shoulders stiffen. I realized that my words had caused unnecessary confusion. They were not meant for him and when I saw him react, it made me feel bad. It was all unintentional, I was not playing games but I had noticed his reaction so I had to set things straight.

'I didn't mean you,' I clarified stupidly and he nodded.

'Did you do something new? Painted today?' he asked. I had taken up painting for the past few days. It was a new hobby, and I was really bad at it but Ronnie didn't care. He loved all my paintings. I wondered how bad a judge of art one had to be to come to such a conclusion.

'Nah! I tried to but I was not inspired enough,' I told him and added, 'I made a new friend, by the way. He lives across the street. His name is Siddharth.'

I saw his face change colour but he schooled his expression in an instant after it gave him away, cleared his throat, and said, 'Great! So how is he?'

'I don't know yet; we had a very funny encounter which involved a drone.' I giggled and told him what had happened. Surprisingly, he looked a little off but was happy that I was happy. I knew him to be protective and jealous at times but now that we were not together, I did not know why I felt a little hurt with his lack of emotion. Maybe I wanted him to get jealous. It was a little twisted of me, to say the least; I wanted him to want me, and yet I wanted him to move on.

I wanted him to tell me he still loved me and then I wanted to reject his love by telling him that I had fallen out of love. Maybe I wanted some revenge or maybe I was still in love with him and just pretending not to be.

I shook my head; it was all so confusing!

'You should talk to people more and try and go out a little after the lockdown is lifted,' he told me, sounding genuine.

'Ya, I will,' I replied absent-mindedly. I will make new friends, I will go out and live my life again, I told myself again after the phone call ended. He had to go and attend to Nani. She was unwell.

I prayed for Nani before pulling my covers over my head. I recalled my time in her house as her PG. The woman was strong and deserved to live a longer and healthier life.

At around ten at night, after tossing in bed for ages, trying to concentrate on a random book on my Kindle, I stretched my arm and picked up the folded paper with Siddharth's number on it. I traced my fingers on the lazily scribbled numbers. It was a little late but I decided to drop him a Hi.

Me: HI, ADIRA HERE

To say that I was not impatient would be wrong. I was impatient. For the last several months, people who had come to me were all known to me. They knew the pre-accident Adira. I could never un-see the pity, the sorrow, the comparisons in their eyes, even Mummy's. I needed someone who would see me as me and talk to me about things without knowing what I had gone through. Therefore I felt that I needed to make new acquaintances and I needed to find new friends.

While I was waiting for Siddharth's response, I received a few baby pictures from Tamanna. Baby Adira engrossed me as she was adorable and my best friend was a hands-on mommy. I smiled watching their antics. Siddharth had still not responded.

Adira

Siddharth, or Sid as he had asked me to call him, is a fun guy. He made me laugh and I heard my laughter echo in the room after ages. I felt like myself again after just one phone call. I am no fool and realized that he was interested in me. However, I made it clear from the word go that I was looking only for friendship with him. Times were tough and I am not only referring to my accident but also to the state of everyone around me. COVID came like a hurricane and uprooted everything. While I was mostly at home, the thrice-a-week visits to my psychotherapist were also cancelled. I was still better off as my mother had funds and papa still transferred a good amount of money to my savings account as my 'pocket money'. I never touch it, but I know it is there if needed.

Sid was like a breath of fresh air in my life. He reminded me of no one in particular and yet he felt like a friend I'd always had. He was shy like Ronnie at times and bashful like Piyush. He gave me my privacy just like Tamanna and was eager to know everything like my mother. After talking to him, I did miss my old life a little more and I had this strange nagging feeling in the pit of my stomach. I wanted to talk to Ronnie.

I could not pinpoint the exact reason why I felt the need to talk to him at two in the night, especially after I had decided on my own to create a little space between us, but I did and there was no reason to it. I checked my phone for a message from him. Would he message me so late at night? I wondered what he was doing at this hour. He was most likely sleeping, with Samba. Ronnie had this habit of slightly drooling while he was asleep, and I loved lifting his chin to close his mouth as he slept. I do not know why but a smile appeared on my face thinking of him splayed across the bed, his arms in all directions and his mouth open enough to let a fly in and out. I could always envision him sleeping peacefully, I could hear his soft breaths and feel his warm arm under my head. No matter how much one tries to get someone out of their head, their heart betrays them. That was exactly what was happening to me. No matter who came into my life, everything reminded me of Ronnie and us. There was no message from him, I stared at the phone for a few moments as my fingers hovered over his number on the screen. I finally gave in; one has to listen to their heart at times and that was exactly what I was doing—I was listening to my heart.

While we forgive others, we need to forgive ourselves too.
We need our own forgiveness as much as we need air to breathe.

Ronnie

It was like 2017 again. I felt a pang of jealousy creep in and flush my face and neck. Time and again, I had told myself that I would let her choose and not influence her choice. I wanted her to come back to me, to remember what we had and give those feelings another chance and I was happy to do that at her pace. I had warned my heart more than a few times that there was a possibility of Adira not taking me back, of her never reciprocating my love and it was okay for her to do so. But that was the moment when I realized how easy it is to feel strong and in control when the situation is hypothetical. The moment another person stepped into the scene, my walls crumbled like a cookie. I was exposed, my feelings were out there to be hurt and despite her telling me that he looked like a friendly guy who meant no harm, I knew the effect she had on me. If I could lose myself in her, someone else could, too. She is the kind of girl many dream of.

It was very easy for me to pretend that there was no other person around her, but her mother and her encounter with Siddharth was one-off because somewhere deep within me, I believed that her moving on from me was not a possibility.

We loved each other and we were meant to be—this was embedded in my heart.

However, the mere mention of another guy who approached her for her phone number brought back the insecure Ronnie. 'Love needs to be giving', 'love is forgiving' and love means to be happy for your loved one even if that means staying out of her life—this is all crap! As she chatted and told me about how it all happened, I tamed my face to look neutral. My hands curled into fists and I could feel my nails digging into my flesh, nearly drawing blood. She looked happy and I was not happy for her. Am I ashamed that I was not feeling the love books tell us about? No! I am not ashamed for feeling the most human feeling. I was feeling jealous and angry and that was love for me. I have always imagined her happiness with me. I knew that I was being a selfish jerk who was only thinking of his happiness but isn't this how humans are? No matter how many times the world tells us, no matter how many times romantic books and songs feed into our heads that true love means to be happy for your loved ones, whether or not we are a part of their lives, we still want their happiness to begin and end with us. We are selfish for we cannot see them happy without us, we cannot find happiness in their happiness alone. I am no different, I am no saint. I want her, I want us; and this new development in her life, even though it was a happy one for her, was not leading towards a 'Happy Us'. And so, I was upset.

When Adira called me, I was over the moon. The conversation started well and slowly it drifted towards Rohit and Sagarika.

'I never heard from either of them,' Adira told me and I went silent for a moment as I knew. I knew that they had been missing but I also knew the reason why. Since the night of the accident, Rohit had time and again repeated that he was responsible for what happened to Adira. Had he taken charge of the situation, things would not have gone so badly. She would not have been lying on the road losing blood. No matter how much I tried to tell him that there are sometimes bigger things at play and we have no control over everything, he couldn't bear to face her.

Sagarika on the other hand had been trying really hard to save her marriage with Rohit. They have been seeking therapy in Delhi and hardly have the time and patience to entertain friends and relatives. As family, we are all trying to give them the space and support that they need to come out of the situation stronger than before. Their start-up, too, was facing the brunt of their domestic issues and had lately become difficult for them to manage.

'They have some issues; they need to sort those out. It's nothing against you,' I told Adira and added, 'I, too, just get a customary message nowadays from Rohit every Diwali and on my birthday. He is a different person now.'

'People change; I have changed so much, too. We have all grown up,' Adira responded and then steered the conversation towards Sid.

I have never been good at hiding what is going on inside me. She could always read me like a book and I love that about her. My happiness morphed into angry jealousy somewhere in the middle of the call and I became quiet.

'Are you upset that I talk to him?' Adira asked and I wanted to scream 'Yes!' But that would have been wrong on my part. Even in the state of mind that I was in, I knew it. 'No! I think you should talk to people more and try and go out a little after the lockdown is lifted,' I said to her as I patted Samba. He had fallen into a deep slumber and was now snoring.

'Samba has gone to sleep and I need to check on Nani, too. Shall I call you tomorrow morning?' I told her and waited with bated breath for her response. Did she want to talk to me the next day? I had to find out. Talking to her all of a sudden felt the same way it felt when I used to talk to her in college—there was an undefinable anticipation, wait, and a sense of insecurity.

'Ya, I will sleep in some time too,' I could hear a smile as she answered. I switched the call to video mode and she switched over. She looked tired with puffy eyes, the room was dark and all I could see clearly was her face bathed in the light from her phone.

'Goodnight, love you,' I said, just as I did every night. Every night she just replied with a 'Goodnight' or sometimes added 'Sweet dreams' and it was enough for me. But not today, I knew that I had been wrong in the past and was getting punished for my own mistakes. But for once I wanted to hear her say that she loved me too. She didn't. She just looked at me, with her big, brown, almond-shaped eyes and whispered a throaty 'Goodnight.'

Unable to think rationally, and not wanting to spoil what was left between us, I disconnected the call. I covered my face with my hands and rubbed my palms over my eyes. A desperate groan escaped my mouth. The world was falling apart for me; the lockdown had taken my parents to a place from where they just could not catch a flight. There were barely enough flights and people fleeing different countries were ready to pay any amount of money to get back home. My parents decided to stay over to help my sister, Nani was so unwell, and I was utterly lonely.

In one's teenage years, we feel that our friends are all that we need, we take the family for granted and the perks that come with living with one's family are not even counted as perks. In a nutshell, we are privileged. But as life happens, your friends move on and they make their own families. That is when you know that friends are not all that we need. We need more—we need our families, we need a partner, we need home-cooked food, we also need our father's lectures, mother's cuddles, grandparents' wisdom-laden anecdotes—a routine in life and so much more.

I missed my parents a lot every time they went to the UK to help their other child, my sister. But never in my life had I been so emotionally drained due to their absence, because every time they went, I knew that if need be I could join them or they me—it is only a seven-hour flight. But it was no longer a seven-hour flight; they were in a different country and we just could not be there for each other. In the same way, I could not be there for Adira no matter how much I wanted to, as she was in another state and the lockdown would keep us apart.

I took Samba to his bed and then walked over to mine. The dog has a serious problem; he just needs to cuddle and thus we eventually ended up in my bed, snuggling. He started snoring again as soon as his head hit the bed but I could not. I was having one of those moments when you seriously want to sleep but your brain has other ideas. The past kept replaying itself in my head and bothering me.

At midnight, I picked up my phone to check the time. Before I could turn the screen off, a number flashed across the screen. It was my Nani's nurse.

'Bhaiya, Nani is unwell and they are taking her to the hospital. They suspect COVID. I will have to go into isolation too if it is COVID,' she said, out of breath as if she was running.

'Who is taking her to the hospital? Don't take her anywhere, I am coming over.' I panicked and Samba woke up startled next to me.

'You cannot, bhaiya. Curfew is in place and the ambulance is here. They won't even let me go with her,' she reasoned.

'I am making a video call on this number, please do not let anyone take her, okay? She has cancer, did you tell them?' I asked, but she had disconnected the call. Frantic, I made a WhatsApp video call on the nurse's number which she picked on the second ring. The video was blurred but I could figure out that she was outside Nani's house.

'Where is Nani? Move the camera towards her, please.' The nurse had a blue mask on. She turned the camera towards an ambulance and I saw Nani hooked on to an oxygen cylinder. Men in PPE kits surrounded her. 'Take me close to her, let me talk to the doctors, please,' I begged the nurse.

'They are not allowing it, bhaiya, they will not hold the phone to avoid contamination. I will ask them in front of you.' She asked the PPE-clad men what would happen next. They were taking Nani to the nearest government hospital as she was unable to breathe on her own. They suspected a COVID infection and asked the nurse to get tested too. Once Nani recovered, they would inform us when to bring her back home.

'She has cancer,' I broke down, telling the nurse to inform them.

'I have told them, bhaiya, that is why it is more important for her to go and get the necessary care as she has a major underlying condition. She will be okay, don't worry,' the nurse consoled me.

As the call disconnected, I felt very uneasy and broken. I didn't know how to help Nani whom my parents had left in my care. There was a lockdown and COVID protocols. If the doctors suspected COVID, they would not let me see her. It was no use chasing the vehicle as that would be illegal. I had to call other family members and tell them what little I knew. I texted Piyush and my sister and calls started flooding my phone. Everyone was as worried and clueless as I was. I don't know when I passed out on the couch, waiting for a call or text from someone.

I woke up at around seven in the morning, my phone had run out of battery and I had a splitting headache. I plugged my phone in and switched it on. As it powered up, I went to the washroom to come back to a buzzing phone. It was an unknown landline number from Delhi.

The pain, anger, loneliness, hurt are a part of me now. Their presence is constant and I only feel detached from them when I sleep. For when I finally sleep, I feel nothing!

Ronnie

My world came crashing down with that one phone call. Nani was no more. She had suffered a heart failure in her sleep the night they had taken her away. My hands shivered as I tried to make sense of what the person on the other end of the call was saying.

I had lost my Nani! I was to take care of her and last night, as she was being taken from her home, I had hoped that she would be back soon. She and I used to joke so many times about beating cancer and neither of us knew that she would leave us all because of something else. COVID caught us all off guard. I offered a silent prayer to god asking him to give peace to Nani's departed soul. She was strict and made us work, but that was her being her. She was a strong woman who used to go for her chemotherapy with a smile on her face and later when she could talk, she would make jokes around it.

'We will cremate her body, it is the protocol . . .' the person on the other end continued, but I was too deep into the emotional turmoil to fully understand his words and tears started filling my eyes, blurring my vision.

'But her children would want to do it! We want to see her one last time. My mother is not even in the country . . .'

'No sir, we will do it the right way, we are not calling to seek permission. It is a call to inform you that we are doing it,' he made it clear to me.

'Let us bring her back to our home at least for the family to see her one last time,' I begged and was told one last time that no one could see her. They had started referring to Nani as the body, and unknowingly, I too by the end of the call was doing the same. It was just the body, after all; the soul, my Nani, had left us for a better place and I was somewhere grateful to god that she didn't have to endure a lot of pain. I cried like a child; I had grown up around her and missed her presence in my life already. I knew that I also had the task of letting everyone else know what had happened but for several minutes, I could do nothing else but cry. The seriousness of the deadly virus had hit me and also the fact that I needed to get tested too as I had visited her in the recent past. Once I was a little composed, I gathered all the courage that I had, to start making the phone calls. Somewhere, I was worried that everyone would blame me, for I was to take care of Nani and I had failed.

My morning was then spent calling and texting relatives to convey the sad news. Everyone was as stunned as I was, but no one blamed me. I had to explain to everyone how and why we couldn't see her one last time, which was the most heartbreaking thing. It was the worst thing for my mother and her siblings—they had, after all, lost their mother, a loss that could never be measured nor be ever compensated for.

By five in the evening, I was so exhausted and emotionally drained that I passed out on the couch.

A phone call woke me up with a jolt. I woke up a little unbalanced and it took me a few seconds to take in my surroundings and recall what had happened in the past twenty-four hours. I picked up my phone to see Adira's number on the screen. She hardly ever called me; it was mostly I who called her nowadays. Fearing the worst, I immediately answered the call. 'Hi,' I said.

'Hey, all okay?' she asked me. Probably my tone gave it away but she knew that something was up and I knew that I had to tell her, too. I just didn't want her to know before all of our family did as it was not about Adira and me; Nani meant a lot of things to a lot of people. Her passing had completely wiped out Adira's concerns from my head for a while. When I didn't call her for one whole day, she knew that something was not okay. I was happy knowing that she still cared and that she could still tell if something was not okay. I felt my throat welling up; it is not easy to come to terms with the loss of a family member. I sat up and placed my elbow underneath me to support my frame. Clearing my throat, I decided to tell her finally, 'No everything is not okay. We . . . we lost Nani,' was all that I could say before I choked again.

'What? How?' Her voice was high-pitched. Naturally, she was shocked.

'COVID, it all happened so suddenly that I didn't even have time to think. She passed away last night in her sleep.'

'Oh Ronnie, I am so sorry. Are you okay? How is Aunty taking it?'

'She will be better as time goes by. Nani was responding so well to chemo, you know. She was in my care, and I let this happen to her. We couldn't even bring her body back home and unknown people have done her cremation. Can you believe that? I feel like I have failed all my family members.' Saying that out loud for the first time, I couldn't control a sob.

'Ronnie, you are not at fault and you know that,' she said. I shook my head. No, I was at fault. I was supposed to be responsible for her all through the lockdown as I was living the closest to her. I had failed everyone, including myself.

'Are you alone now?' she asked me in a concerned voice.

'Samba is here, everyone else is stuck where they are.' Never in my life had I missed my family so much. We could talk to each other for hours but could not be there even though we wanted to.

'Come over,' she said in a hushed tone.

'It is not possible.' I knew that she knew it too, but it was so good to hear her say it to me as if she meant it.

'I am so sorry, Ronnie . . .' she said.

'No, I am sorry, baby. I am sorry for every time I took you or anyone for granted, I am sorry for keeping my emotions within me and not expressing myself. I am sorry for not valuing you enough. I am sorry for being in love but not saying it enough and I am sorry for all the wrongs that I did to you. I know sorry doesn't make anything right, but I am sorry nevertheless.' Emotions took hold of my thoughts and in that instant, I felt completely alone in the world.

'Sometimes things happen in life for us to get clarity on our priorities. Certain accidents make us better people.' I knew she was talking about her accident and I wanted to scream at her and say that she'd nearly lost her life because of me and I could never forget that.

'No, lessons for me should not have nearly cost you your life. You are being too soft on me.' That was the most that we had ever spoken about the accident. Most of the time when I wanted to talk, it was just me asking for forgiveness and she changing the topic to one of our friends or Samba.

And, as expected, Samba cropped up in the conversation. 'How is Samba? Have you guys eaten something?' I had not and Samba had been living off milk since last night.

'No,' I told her blankly as the furry pug took the cue at the mention of his name and crawled into my lap. He was being overly quiet as if he too sensed something was wrong. I think he knew that Nani was no longer with us. Dogs always know . . .

'Eat something, I shall call you again in one hour to check,' she told me and we disconnected the call.

An hour later I called her, but her phone was busy. I knew she had found a new lockdown friend, and no matter what I told her, I was not okay with it any more. I wanted her to be back in my life. We were meant to be. We knew each other so well, cared for one another, and had an unexplainable connection. That was the moment when I decided to end my half-hearted efforts and give it all that I had.

Some fifteen minutes went by with no callback. I was tired and emotional, the warm Maggi noodles in my belly did the trick and I closed my eyes to sleep even though I could see her number flash on my phone's screen. I could not talk in that state.

Did you ever think that meeting people would be a privilege?
Talking to someone would make you realize that you were still alive?
That you still matter?
Loneliness is hollowing; it makes one empty. It is draining and it
takes away all that one has.

Ronnie

The next several days of the lockdown were painful, to say the least. With Nani gone, I had no reason to ever step outside the house at all. Adira and I spoke a lot and revisited the past. While my aim was for her to fall in love with me again, I found myself drowning in my love for her, memories and her. While I would want to consider that I was making some progress with her, the fact that her new friend was wooing her with the latest technology burnt my insides.

The guy and Adira had not met in person yet, but they used to talk a lot and text. Adira is not on social media any more, so he sends her jokes and memes that are new to her and she then forwards them to me—which is obnoxious and I usually do not know whether to laugh or cry at them. Taking advantage of the virtual world, I too went on a few virtual dates with her. It was not the same as going out with her, but we did fairly well. Our first virtual date was a Maggi noodles date.

On the seventeenth day of the lockdown, we made a bowl of Maggi each, dimmed our bedroom lights and I made a video call to her on WhatsApp. Honestly, I was feeling giddy and in the pit of my stomach I had a new sensation, a feeling

I had never experienced before and can only describe as sharp and tingling. As I have mentioned many times before, I was in love with her more than ever and I knew that there was some competition around even though Adira kept saying that Sid was just a friend and he knew that I existed. How could I tell her that I was aware that her parents had found a boy for her in 2016. It was when we were all in college. The information had sparked fury in my head; it made me look for ways to make her fall in love with me sooner and I believed that only magic could help me, black magic to be specific. I went to meet a conman who asked me to get thirty strands of her hair so that he could perform a love-voodoo on Adira. I had stooped really low and was on my way to collect her hair from her trash when luckily I heard Tamanna's voice and the fear of getting caught saved me from doing something that I would have been ashamed of all my life. But I did know that I would have done it, I would have, in fact, done anything to make her love me back. I would have stooped lower than anything one could imagine. And if I could do it, I knew someone else could do it too for a girl like her.

Anyway, I placed my phone on the table and we started talking. The topic, to begin with, was how my Maggi was plain while she had made herself a cheesy Maggi. She was cooking again and happiness was evident all over her face. She was happy with something in her life and I prayed that it was the fact that she and I were getting back together. More than anything else I hoped it was not Sid.

'How was your day?' I asked, cocking an eyebrow and she laughed. A burst of laughter reached her eyes and my heart.

'It was good actually. I spoke to Tamanna; she is very busy with little Adira.' She forked her noodles and a few strands of hair fell on her face. She had let her hair loose that day and I was the happiest to look at her face occupying my phone's screen.

'Ya, I know, right! Piyush hardly has any time nowadays even for a phone call. At least Tamanna spoke to you,' I said. I was not upset with Piyush for not calling that much any more. I was happy as they were both moving on in their lives.

'I could never imagine them being parents especially after what I witnessed the day of my accident,' she said.

'What did you see?' I asked, filling my mouth with a forkful of noodles. She told me about the fight she had accidentally witnessed.

'There are all kinds of couples in the world, Adira. Some never fight and are always on the same page and then some fight like cats and dogs but still cannot live apart from each other. Tamanna and Piyush are the cats and dogs kind,' I explained. 'No two love stories are alike, no two couples are alike either.'

'What kind of couple were we, Ronnie?' See, I told you she and I were heading somewhere; she had started talking about the past now even though she just used a word that killed me on the inside—'were'—the past, I was her past.

Ignoring the pang I said, 'We are the ones who could not be away from each other. I am the jerk in the relationship and you are my angel. We are destined to be together, we are to be present in each other's lives. Maybe as friends or something else, I don't know. All that I know is that we complete each other and we have to be with each other after all the ups and downs. So, we are the destined couple.' I bared all my teeth in the end, to add humour to the statement. I wanted her to feel my emotions but I didn't want her to stop talking to me altogether because I was moving at a faster pace which might have been uncomfortable for her.

'Sid said the same,' she said and shocked me, to say the least. I gulped some water; I needed to quench my thirst. I was parched after her bold statement.

'What? He said this about us?' I was not sure what were we talking about here.

'He says that he feels I am a part of his life for a reason and no matter what happens, we will always be a part of each other's life. He is a very nice boy. He never lived his life for himself and I am glad that he can now live some part of it with me.' She sounded genuine but I was furious. I had just stopped thinking about stooping low and there it was! A prime example! Maybe they were friends but they hardly knew each other to make such statements!

I stuffed my face with Maggi so that I would not say something that would cost me more than what I would gain by bashing this guy. We ate in silence for some time and then her mother walked into our date, 'Adira, you are not done yet? I thought you had to sleep early today!'

'Namaste, Aunty,' I said, as was customary, and she just nodded in acknowledgement.

'Ya Mummy, we are almost done,' Adira told her mother.

We were done? No! I had so many things that I had to talk about. I wanted to say so many things, hear so many things, talk about this Sid guy too. But Aunty was Aunty.

'I might move close to you after the lockdown,' the abrupt statement fell from my mouth. There was a non-concrete plan—it was more of a thought bubble really, but now it was out in the open. So there had to be a concrete plan in place.

'Really?' was Adira's response and 'Why?' came from her mother.

Ignoring the older lady, I nodded and added, 'I just need a place to live really, where Samba is not a bother either.'

'We do not keep PGs,' her mother chimed in.

This woman had just crashed our date uninvited and was now getting on my nerves. 'We can keep Samba for you and then you can look for a regular PG,' said Adira, who had always wanted to keep Samba since Nani was not well and I used to take him to her every weekend. With Nani's passing away, I knew that she wanted to be his new mommy. Having Samba there would mean I would be there most of the days too. It was indeed a perfect plan.

'How will you manage your job?' Aunty wanted me either to react or was genuinely concerned. I would put my money on the latter.

'I can work from home for many months at a time, the company allows it.' *Really? Does it?* I so wanted to kick myself for the web of lies that I had started spinning.

'Adira, I am getting your medicines. End the call soon.' She finally walked out of the room switching on the lights on her way out and successfully ending our virtual date night.

'You know, Ronnie, this sounds good. If you can move here, it will be good for you too, especially because your family is away. Mummy can cook you dinner every night,' she winked.

I added nothing else—her mother might slowly poison me through those dinners. Adira knew that too.

But I had other things to worry about, like the work-from-home set-up I had just bragged about.

Adira

When you hear of someone passing away, it is sad, no matter whether you knew them enough or not, whether you liked them enough or not. Apart from the fact that the news is sad, it is also in a way jolting because each one of us till then takes their time on the planet for granted. My memories from the accident had still not left me and then the news of Ronnie's Nani passing away arrived. The world was not the same with the pandemic and this bit of news jolted me.

It is funny how when we are in distress or when we are scared, we want to be with people we love the most. I had believed till this moment that I didn't love anyone other than my mother and, of course, myself. But I was so wrong, my heart ached to be with Ronnie and pacify him. He sounded broken and alone. But I couldn't go to him even if I wanted to. The world was locked, people were dying and we just couldn't go anywhere as per our whims and fancies. Moreover, I didn't love Ronnie any more—I reasoned with myself. I knew it was a lie; I did love him, probably not all of him but definitely a version of him that was frozen in my memory. This stupid feeling of love was just hiding somewhere deep within my heart. Sometimes the matters of the heart get complex; there is this constant battle with oneself that one cannot escape. I was in the middle of nowhere at a constant battle that would not resolve itself without any effort.

Honestly, it feels awful to miss a person like that. You think that someone is out of your life, that you are ready to move on after you have been hurt enough and grieved over and over again and then . . . bam! They are all over your thoughts again. You miss them again, you crave to be with them again. But life doesn't give many people second chances. I had planned to do as I wanted to, to act upon every impulse without much thought. And yet I could not ignore the constant dull pain in my heart. I knew that I was longing to see him. *Where would it lead us?* I didn't want to give it a thought just yet. All I knew was that I had to see him if I couldn't be with him, so I made a call, a video call, and he instantly picked it up as if he had been waiting for me to make the move, as if he had been waiting for me to decide.

Ronnie's face flashed on my screen and my heart raced. It was stupid really, I was not a teenager to feel like that. I shook my head and looked at his face again, his eyes had dark circles underneath them and he looked tired.

'How are you?' I asked, even though we had spoken just a while ago.

'The same,' he said. 'How are you feeling?'

Ronnie

Adira never initiated a video call so as soon as I saw her number flash on the screen, I got worried. I picked the call before the second ring and was relieved to see her face. She was lying in bed and her bedside lamp had bathed her face in a golden light. I could see the scar on the left side of her forehead. The stitches had left a mark there. Other than that, her face was as perfect as it had been the day I'd first seen her. When her mother had told me that she needed to rest, I, too, had retired to bed. I was tired and my body hurt after so much emotional turmoil through the day but looking at her, I forgot all that I had been through.

'How are you feeling?' I asked her and she smiled as she said, 'Confused.'

'Confused? What happened?' The first thought in my head was of Sid.

'Nothing,' she shook her head and her dark hair fell on her face. As she lifted her hand to tuck it away, I saw how empty her wrist looked without the bracelet. She had started wearing her emerald ring again, though.

'Did you take your medicines?' I asked her, taking my mind off the temptation to ask her if she missed the bracelet.

'Yes, I did. How have you been coping? I was worried for you.' This made me feel warm. Knowing that she still cared even just as a friend. Since the accident, she spoke at a slow pace, trying to cover the slight stutter. I could feel that every time she paused after a word or sighed before beginning a sentence.

'I will show you something.' The moment the words slipped out of my mouth I knew that I was doing something really stupid; it was all so premature. But I have a foot-in-mouth problem and I couldn't not go ahead with what I had started. So I picked up the bracelet from the top of my bedside table and dangled it in front of the screen. 'This suits you,' I said, not looking her in the eye. I was worried that maybe I had taken the concern in her voice for something else.

'Oh my God! How did you get it?' She asked me, wide-eyed. Was she not aware that her mother had thrown it at my face one day when I had visited her at the hospital and told me never to come close to Adira ever again? Maybe not; what person would describe such a cruel act to their child even if it was done to protect them.

'Your mother had it, it was handed over to her by the doctors when you were in the hospital,' I informed her carefully, editing the details of how exactly the scene unfolded.

'I thought that it was lost during . . . you know the . . . ac . . . accident but it survived.' Her eyes pooled in the corners and I hated the sight. Whether she was crying tears of sorrow or joy didn't matter, they were tears nevertheless.

'Barely, this barely survived. It was broken at the clasp and charms were missing.' *It was broken just like our . . .* I wanted to add.

'I got it repaired for you but never had the guts to bring it along. It would have opened wounds,' I confessed, playing with the charms on the bracelet.

'Why? I want it back. It belongs to me and neither Mummy nor you have the right to keep it away from me,' she said, pouting like a stubborn child. She was still looking at the bracelet in awe with her furrowed eyebrows. I had almost forgotten how big her eyes were and how dreamy they looked at night. I could think of every possibility swimming in those eyes; they could make me do things I would regret, say things that were not appropriate. So, I focused on the bracelet instead.

'Bring it along when you come here,' she instructed, breaking the spell.

'Yes I will, you sleep now,' I told her half-heartedly as I knew that she needed rest to recover and also because I didn't want to say and feel things that I had no right to. I was under her spell, and she knew it.

'Mmm . . . I will sleep. Where is Samba?' She kept asking me questions, making me fall deeper into her world.

She wanted to know everything now—how was I planning to move to Chandigarh while the lockdown was in place, did I get the work-from-home approvals, what would be my living arrangements while in the city, did I want to stay close to her to keep an eye on her? Was Samba to come along, too, at the same time? How was my sister doing? When was the second baby due? How was the app coming along? And a million other things.

So, our call lasted till the early hours of the morning. I was not complaining, not at all. I was happy to be talking to her like nothing had happened between us, but the reality was that a lot had transpired and we were not a couple any more. While she didn't have any other man in her life, I knew that I would be in a mess emotionally if we kept talking the way we were. But I still couldn't just disconnect the call. I didn't dare do so. I couldn't break my own heart, which was again weaving dreams of a life with her.

Life is so fulfilling when you accept that you can never control anything. It is a free fall and all you can do before your time is up is to enjoy the journey. The fall is beautiful, exhilarating, but out of our control.

Ronnie

Time and again I have been made aware by life that I am not a superhero. My wishes are not above the law or nature. No matter what plans I make, they seldom become a reality. While I had abruptly planned that I was going to move my base to Chandigarh, would magically find a place to stay within my budget during the pandemic, and thus would get to meet Adira every day, my life had other plans. After more than a dozen calls to people who had time and again boasted of their magical skills of getting work done, I realized that it was not child's play to firstly get an exception to move across state borders during the twenty-one-day lockdown. All the promises of '*Bhai, tere liye kuch bhi*' (Anything for you, brother) failed the test of time.

So I was stuck in Delhi with only my companion who loved to snore underneath my bed. My sister had a son during the same time and I became an uncle once again. It was a little embarrassing to tell Adira further details on the move mainly because her mother gloated right next to her. I could feel my ears burning every time she made sure she asked me where I was on my plans to move.

'I am trying, Aunty,' I said on every occasion and she looked as if she was genuinely worried for me, for my being alone in Delhi. Piyush, too, kept on checking with me every other day despite his busy life. His phone calls were now also regular as we were approaching the end of the initial phase of our start-up, TeachMee. Tamanna was now fully involved and kept pestering me to ask Adira to get on board as she was amazing with client management and soon we would need a client manager. We were funding the project out of our own pockets and it was a very ambitious one. Getting a resource from outside was out of the question. I too wanted Adira on board but I did not want her to overwork and coming to us in the initial phase meant a lot of work and no pay. But I did promise Tamanna that I would ask her, I would ask her as soon as I felt the time was right. On the subject of the app, let me tell you how it all began:

The App

Right before the pandemic struck, we had a school get-together. While we had invited our entire batch, only seven boys and three girls turned up. It is the story of most get-togethers, I guess. With very few in attendance, we soon ran out of topics from our present life and started revisiting the past. The most obvious topics were our teachers. My best friend from school, Nimit, still lived in his old house which was right behind the school campus. As soon as he shared the information, it was unanimously decided that we should visit his house and try and sneak into the old building. The only two girls in attendance—Archana and Priyanka—immediately called their respective spouses and left. They didn't want to get caught sneaking into the building and thought we had all lost our minds.

We didn't grieve over the loss of two of our soldiers and continued with our plan. After all, it was not the first time we would be sneaking into the building without permission, but who was to tell those girls and scare the living daylights out of them? They were frontbenchers who knew nothing about the world of backbenchers. As responsible grown men, we stayed with the two women until their partners arrived, keeping them entertained with silly jokes and old memories. Memories are magical things. While time keeps moving forward and you think that nothing can be the same again, memories can prove you wrong in a second. The moment we all started revisiting the old times, it felt as if time had stood still and we could see through the window of memories and relive our childhood once again.

After around half an hour of non-stop chatter, the girls left our company and all the boys decided that it was time to visit the old school. Our first stop was Nimit's house. His parents welcomed us initially but as soon as they realized that we were all at least two beers down each, they asked Nimit to kick us out. It was just like the old times! After school, we used to crash at Nimit's home as both his parents were working. It was all fun and frolic until his mother came back from work and then we were kicked out in no time on account of creating unnecessary ruckus.

As we had nowhere to go, we picked up some more beer and headed towards our next destination—our school. The lights of the school building were on and there was someone in the guard room. I clearly remember that there was no guard there after four in the evening, all through the time we studied there. This was a new development which could have meant that we were going back home or anywhere else but not inside the school. Then, much to our surprise, we didn't have to find a way to break in.

While the timing for the guard had changed, the guard in the guard room was still the same, Sachin Bhaiya. His name was Sachin Tyagi but we always referred to him as Sachin Bhaiya. He recognized us after a few references were given to him. 'Achcha! I know who you guys are!' he said, baring his tobacco-stained teeth. I did not believe him. I think he just knew that Nimit was a neighbour and was being kind to us. We hugged him one by one because even if he didn't remember who we were, he was a part of our childhood that we were there to revisit. He let us in without any question and opened all the doors for us.

'You come along too please, Sachin Bhaiya, we have beer,' said Rohit Banga. Sachin Bhaiya, who now had a teenage son, put his son in charge of the guard cabin and tagged along. Once inside, we spoke non-stop, sometimes even all together at once. There were so many memories—this was where we used to hide during morning assembly. Look at the staff room, nothing has changed! The principal's office was where no one wanted to go. Remember the time when we used to be standing out for all the periods? We never did our homework. And the chemistry lab blast? No one knows that Sakshi was behind it! This tree was for lovers only. This was our lunch spot and so on and so forth!

We spent hours roaming around the school and revisiting memories, or maybe it was just one hour. I was a little high and keeping time was difficult. We had met each other at five in the evening and it was dark outside by the time we walked into the building. Soon, the fit men that we were, we started feeling a heaviness in our steps. We were all tired, so Sachin Bhaiya opened the doors of the auditorium for us. This space was built after we had left school and was new for us; there were no memories. We just slumped on the seats and looked around in wonder. But eight drunk men, alone inside a big building, cannot keep quiet. Thus it began, we started discussing the teaching staff.

Nimit knew the whereabouts of most of them and so did Sachin Bhaiya for obvious reasons. 80 per cent of our teachers were still teaching at the school while the rest had retired. Our maths teacher, Makhija Sir, had passed away a few years ago. He was a nice man who had lived a fulfilling life. We recalled how he used to pester us and make us solve problems in front of the whole class on the blackboard. I was neither an exceptionally bright nor a dumb student as far as academics went.

'Sunita Ma'am had the worst fate,' Sachin Bhaiya said, taking a big chug out of his bottle and we all looked at him. Sunita Ma'am was our chemistry teacher and was great at what she taught. Her examples made the thickest brain remember and understand chemistry equations. He took his own time, savouring the liquid before he continued, 'She retired and took tuitions for several years before losing her sight. The tuitions stopped and her son and daughter-in-law threw her out on the streets to beg. Someone found her and took her to the hospital. Some students' families footed the bill, but she had no place to go after she recovered. Then they set up a small fund for her. Her vision was so poor that she was unable to cook or take care of herself. Soon she died.' He took another sip and we all looked at each other.

'Did you know about this?' I asked Nimit in wonder. We had all been in touch with each other via social media and even though none of us was very rich, we earned enough to have been able to support her had we known. Nimit shrugged and said he didn't know anything about it either.

I was not completely sloshed by the beer but was shaken by the news. That was when I decided I had to do something to help our teachers. I did not know how or what had to be done, but I could not just let it be a piece of news and move on in life. Soon the topic changed to other things and I lost track mainly because my mind kept wandering back to Sunita Ma'am.

Once home, I called Adira. She was awake and reading a book. She knew that I was going out with my classmates so naturally she asked me how it went. I could not resist telling her about Sunita Ma'am. 'What do you want to do? Set up a fund?' she asked me and I started thinking if that was the best thing to do. 'I do not think many teachers would like to opt for charity. They have a lot of self-respect and moreover, it is not easy to make people donate for causes that easily.'

'Then create a source of income for them, similar to a royalty payment,' she said and we wondered together what could be done to ensure a lifelong income for these teachers. I didn't want her to stay up till very late, so I insisted that we brainstorm the next day.

While I lay awake in bed that night, I came up with an idea. Some of the teachers are so good that new teachers could learn from them, from the way they could make tricky topics accessible. So, what if the teachers had an option of recording their teachings like a YouTube video, which would be available via an app? This video could be paid for and we could pay out royalty. The royalty amount would depend on the number of views a video received. These learning videos could be played for an entire classroom, an individual student, new teachers, etc. Thinking of how and what, I dozed off.

In the morning when I woke up, thankfully, I still had my idea intact in my head. I sent a text to Piyush and he called me within a few hours. His wife was also on board now. Adira came up with the name TeachMee and Tamanna was happy to help with resources. And just like that, within a few hours, TeachMee was born.

Ronnie

Coming back to the present . . .

The only thing that came true from the initial plan was my wish to see Adira every day. Nowadays, she video-called me every night, sometimes after her mother went off to bed and we talked about everything under the sun for long hours. If her mother was around, we spoke less and our conversation was limited to her day and my day, nothing beyond that. When we could speak to each other without the older woman present, Adira giggled at my lame jokes and I enjoyed seeing her, but mostly I missed looking at her in person. When I went back to working in mid-2019, Rajbir was senior manager and had moved out of my department. I was assigned to a new team and a new manager. He was a very understanding man and did not mind my frequent visits to Chandigarh as long as I was available to finish the jobs assigned to me. When COVID-19 was declared a pandemic, my colleagues and I were informed by my new manager that all the employees were expected to work remotely. Despite the announcement that the lockdown would be lifted soon, I had no plans as to how I would move to Chandigarh. I had called more than a few realtors who had listed properties on OLX but none was in my budget. My salary allowed me only enough money to fulfil my responsibilities towards my parents. Since I had started working, I had never asked anyone for money and I didn't want to start then either. I had to find a solution that was within my means. So I called Piyush for help.

'I need to find someone who can keep me as a paying guest as I do not think that I can manage to take up a whole house on rent. Houses in Chandigarh are too expensive,' I told him.

'For how long?' he asked me, trying to pacify the wailing baby in his arms at the same time. Baby Adira sure was in possession of very healthy lungs. She was screaming the house down and her father sounded too cool. If I had not known already, it was easy to assume that she had her father's blood.

'I will see what I can do but I cannot promise anything at this stage,' he told me before his daughter went into full-blown screaming for something that the new father had yet to figure out. 'Do you want this?' he said over the phone; the question was not for me, one did not need to be a genius to figure that. 'Tamannaaaaa,' he screamed and that was my cue.

'I will call tomorrow,' I told him and immediately hung up the call.

Surprisingly, within minutes, my phone rang and Piyush's number flashed across the screen. I was in the middle of changing my clothes so I quickly threw a T-shirt on and answered the call.

'So listen,' he began and told me that Tamanna's new boss Mr Sharma's parents lived very close to Adira's mother's house. She had casually mentioned that to him once. Just before the lockdown was imposed, he had moved there to live with his ageing parents as he was their only child. Though they were pretty sure they were not in need of a paying guest, Tamanna had asked her boss if he could help out and he offered an accommodation to me at no cost for two weeks. This was to be on the condition that I move into my own space by the end of two weeks. Sometimes when you think that there is no hope and you cannot control a situation, the universe surprises you. I offered a silent prayer to the universe.

'Do they know that I will have a dog with me?' I asked Piyush.

'Are you seriously planning to make Samba travel? He is old now and he need not run around the world with you. Leave him with the neighbours. I do not think that Tamanna's boss will be able to accommodate two dogs in the house for two weeks,' he told me laughing, naturally hinting that I was one of the dogs that he was referring to. Ignoring his remark, I informed him that Samba was indeed travelling with me and so was my car. If Mr Sharma did not like dogs, then Samba would have to live with Adira's mom but I could not burden the neighbours with his responsibility. Nor could I leave him with a stranger or a friend as he was indeed an aged dog who liked doing things as per his whims and fancies. Now that Nani was gone, he was my responsibility, and I would place him with someone who loved him as much as Nani did. Only Adira fit that bill. So I called her and asked if she was okay with him living with her until I found a place for both of us to settle in.

Adira was on her terrace when I called her. Her new friend Sid had been paying a visit to her house every day. 'He is a decent chap and he is just looking for someone his age to talk to. He is also Mum's friend's son. We are like family friends now,' she told me. Ya, right! Someone his age was spending some quality time with a girl who was not just fascinating and beautiful but charming beyond compare. I could not tell her how much I wanted to kill this guy, so much so that I had more than ten ideas on how to effectively murder him swimming in my head every time she mentioned that he was there to visit her or had called late at night.

'I have found a family that is happy to give me some space in their house for the first fourteen days, but I do not wish to burden them with Samba's presence too. You know how he thinks of himself as royalty; he likes to make people run around for him and do all his chores,' I told her, petting the one I was talking about. He made a gruff noise in agreement.

'No, not at all! I would love to keep him. I adore him and you know that. Moreover, I had been longing to see him and spend some time with him. It seems like forever that I got to pat him. I miss him,' she told me happily and I was relieved.

'Will your mother allow it?' I asked her with doubts bursting into my thoughts. Her mother didn't like me and naturally, her emotions overflowed and touched everything and everyone that was connected to me. She once adored Tamanna but since she'd become my sister-in-law, Adira's mother despised her. Once, she even said that her husband had done some black magic on her which was why she was not the same girl that she had been when she was single. She called her a girl who had lost track of her life and submitted to her husband when she could have been happier and more successful had she chosen someone else as a partner. She was cold towards Piyush as well. Every time I took Samba to meet Adira, her mother complained a lot about the amount of hair he shed and called him a hairball bomb—not lovingly, of course!

'I will manage Mummy. You don't know it but she asked me if I wanted a puppy. Every time she sees a pug she asks the owner if they are planning to breed more or if they have a litter. She might look and behave as if she doesn't love or care but she does. More than you know . . .'

I wondered if her mother would one day like me too, or just be okay with me being around her. Or was her liking just limited to the dog? My eyes moved to find Samba and I wondered if he was normal. While he had been chasing his tail clockwise for the past several minutes, he decided to change direction and run anti-clockwise after the tail. *Can one love and hate someone at the same time?* I was feeling both the feelings for the dog chasing its tail in front of me. He was adorable but I was filled with hatred for him all of a sudden because he had managed to do what I couldn't. Lucky bastard! He would get to live with Adira and her mother and would be making his way into their hearts while I would be crazily looking for accommodation for both of us.

The next two days flew by as I packed and prepared. On the third day, I took a day off, packed three more small bags, dumped them in the boot, and made the four-hour journey in six hours to Chandigarh. I had never lived away from my house for long and whenever I had, I had my mother to help me out with packing. I was a grown man and it is indeed nothing to be proud of, but when one lives in a house all their life with their mother, they are kind of dependent on her. My parents still owned a beat-up Maruti Zen. I had never bothered to get another car of my own. There had been no need as I mostly took the metro to work and Papa still had his Vespa scooter for when I wanted to meet friends. I didn't want to overheat the old car. So, Samba and I took frequent breaks, and our journey extended by two more hours.

When we reached our destination, we were both tired, exhausted, hungry, and I was in need of a shower. I straightaway headed to Adira's door. I had travelled all day and could be carrying COVID-19 germs. So, I pulled a mask on my face, pulled Samba out of the car, and texted Adira.

WE ARE HERE, COME AND TAKE YOUR BOY INSIDE

Cheeky? I know, right, but it was okay once in a while I guess. I was expecting a grinning girl to open the door but to my surprise, her mother came out to pick up Samba instead. She had a mask on through which she said, 'You must be carrying a lot of germs; did you sanitize your hands before holding the leash? Is the leash clean? When did he last bathe? Why is he panting?'

There were way too many questions, and I was just too tired to respond to her remarks, so I just randomly nodded my head not bothering to reply to any. My eyes roamed to the space behind her as I tried to peek into the house. She knew who I was looking for.

'She has a friend over, a boy. His name is Siddharth. He is a manager in a big firm. Did you get a promotion yet?'

Of course, I could see what she was trying to do but I didn't react. I just counted from one till ten and calmed my nerves. 'I shall come to meet her in the evening,' I declared and turned on my heel. Samba, the unfaithful dog, followed her inside wagging his tail. 'Traitor,' I muttered under my breath and started the car. The next stop was the Sharma residence and I was so grateful to them, for being willing to help an unknown man during such times.

Sometimes good luck is hidden in bad luck and sometimes bad luck is hidden in good luck.
It is all a part of life. It is all a part of the game.

Ronnie

After an encounter with her mother, I was too tired to care about the man who was in Adira's company. I made my way to Mr Sharma's house. It was not very far from Adira's mother's home and the distance gave me some pleasure. It would be fairly easy to come over more than once a day, I thought, and started weaving dreams as I dragged my feet up to my temporary residence's door. I didn't get all my stuff out of the car as I had decided not to scare the generous people. I had over-packed and if I had to give you an outsider's viewpoint, it appeared that I was moving houses instead of moving in temporarily. I rang the doorbell and birds chirped. That was not unusual; our neighbours had the same doorbell. It was indeed a blessing that Samba was not to live there as he could never control himself around loud doorbells.

A few moments after ringing the bell, just when I was thinking of pressing the button again, a woman came to the door to let me in. I introduced myself and she smiled at me before letting me know that they were expecting me. That was Mrs Sharma, a woman who was my mother's age. I bent down to touch her feet and she ever so lightly placed her palm on my head muttering her blessings. Mr Sharma joined us and I followed the same process. 'You travel very light. We were told that you are to stay here for two weeks,' the gentleman joked. I told him that I didn't want to bring all my luggage inside in one go.

'There is a lot of stuff in the car, Uncle,' I told him and he cracked a joke about how his wife carries everything right from a pen to a chopping board on their trips. They were a nice couple and after our interaction, I realized that my time there could be memorable in their company. I was shown into a decently furnished bedroom.

'I would like to pay for my stay, Uncle,' I told him as he showed me the attached washroom. 'I cannot take advantage of your kindness,' I added.

'You are just like our son and we have been told that you need the space for only two weeks. We cannot accept any money. Just be nice, keep the room clean and keep praising Mrs Sharma's food!' he joked with a wink and left me in the room without taking up my offer.

I was now missing my parents much more than I usually did. So, I moved in a couple of bags and sent a message to my sister to check if they were all free for a video call. There was no response from her for some time, so I took a quick shower. By the time I walked out of the bathroom, there were three missed calls and a few messages from her. The last one had come in a few moments ago. I dialled her number and finally got to see my family after a while. They all looked healthy and happy, including the kids. 'I think you are making it very difficult for yourself, you have lost so much weight,' my concerned mother said and made me laugh.

'You think that I am losing weight all the time, Mummy. Look at this,' I tried to flex my muscles in front of the camera and it was my sister's turn to roll on the floor laughing.

'Those are not muscles, *yeh masle hain inka hal dhoondo* (these are problems that need a solution),' she said and naturally everyone else laughed along with her.

'Ha ha, very funny! You think of your own tummy, *motu* (fatty),' I teased her and our brother–sister banter continued for a while.

'How is Adira?' Papa asked me and everyone went quiet.

'She is better now. I am yet to meet her,' I told them all. We chatted for a bit and then I bid them all goodbye.

My mood was elevated and could feel happiness fill me after seeing my family. I put on a grey T-shirt with a collar, dark blue denims, then slipped my shoes on, and headed out of the room. Mrs Sharma, like all mothers, was concerned about my food. She reminded me that I had not eaten for many hours and it made sense to fill my rumbling tummy with some of her home-cooked food. That was the moment when I was also told that I was living with a pure vegetarian family and they would let me stay only if I followed the same food rules. Looking at the delicious poha in front of me, I had no trouble accepting. After all, it was only going to be for a few days. I checked my watch and realized that the entire day had just flown by, and I had not done a single thing that I had planned to do. I had not met Adira yet, I had not even drafted a business proposal for two prospective investors for TeachMee. Tamanna would be after my case that evening as she had high hopes of getting funding from a US-based angel investment company. Putting aside the horrifying thoughts of Tamanna strangling the life out of me, I told Mrs Sharma that I would be gone for some time to meet a friend. 'Do not meet a lot of people, and sanitize your hands before you touch our doorbell. Take a shower as soon as you come back. What time will you come?' She gave me a series of instructions.

'An hour, hour and a half maximum,' I told her, pretty sure that Adira's mother would not let me stay with her any longer than that.

'My son should be back by then, too,' she told me and I nodded. I was yet to meet and greet the younger Mr Sharma and thank him for his and his family's generosity. Mr Sharma had some work in the neighbourhood so while we were in the same vicinity, we had not met yet. Tamanna had given me strict instructions to be nice and leave a parting gift as a sign of my gratitude. More than my manners, it was my fear of her that forced me to stay in check most of the time as well as on this occasion. I informed Mrs Sharma that I was looking forward to meeting her son and stepped out of the house to meet Adira.

Adira and her mother lived in a double-storey house, which was spacious and too big for just two women to live in. I had spent enough time in the house to know that there were more than three bedrooms that remained unoccupied at any given time. I wondered if her mother might, after all, agree to let me stay there. It would be the perfect place for me to live for the rest of the time that I could work from anywhere. I decided to be nice to her and see if she would give in to my charm. Whether I had any charm in me or not was something I wanted to think a lot about.

For a change, the doorbell was answered by Adira and my face lit up. She wore a light pink kurti and white salwar. A blue mask was dangling from her left ear and she grinned at me. Swiftly she secured her mask on her face while I stood there staring at her. Her long hair was longer than what I remembered. She was wearing several silver bangles on her right hand that made a beautiful tingling noise every time she made even the slightest movement. Not only did Adira smile at me but she also gave me a light hug as we met. It was a friendly gesture but was enough to send my heart racing. I could not help an ugly blush creep up on me. It was embarrassing, so I decided not to look into her eyes and focused on her feet instead. She was not wearing shoes, her nails were painted red and looked lovely. Suddenly, it occurred to me that I was wearing a mask; the blush was hidden and I felt my confidence returning. I grinned like a monkey underneath the mask even as she turned around to lead the way. As she turned, my eyes fell on the ॐ tattoo at the nape of her neck, as she had moved her hair to one side. I observed that her limp was less prominent as I followed her into the house, sanitizing my hands, thinking about her, about us, about our past, about our future.

Just when I was getting too ahead of myself, I saw him sprawled on the sofa with his hand leisurely resting on the hand rest. A tall, broad man with a well-trimmed beard, he was talking animatedly to Adira's mother and the old woman was blushing or laughing or doing both. Under his feet lay the animal who was supposed to die saving my life—Samba—keeping all his loyalty at bay and enjoying himself as his tummy was being caressed by the man's feet. But he was doing nothing that was expected of him. Samba was on the floor, under that man's feet enjoying his feet caress him. I knew pugs are not known for their loyalty but this one was a disgrace to his race.

'This is Sid,' Adira said to me as if I had to be told. This man was just as I had envisioned him. Good-looking, confident, and everything that I was not. How could anyone think that he was there only to be friends with this girl? There had to be more to it. He was not blind. Maybe it was not me but this guy who was the reason Adira was extra happy and improving day by day. I should have been happy for her—I had promised that to myself but I was not. I was anything but happy for any of them and my heart tore into pieces.

As soon as we walked in, Sid looked at us. Just as I could tell it was him by the way he was sitting, he too could tell who I was. I felt that in his gaze. Adira had mentioned more than once that she and Sid did talk about me. He knew me as her friend, he knew me as her past. He smiled at me warmly or maybe he smiled at Adira and I was in the way. Nevertheless, I had to be the gentleman just as he was, especially because both Adira and her mother were there. So, I extended my hand for a handshake. His grip was firm, which was no surprise and we introduced ourselves to each other. Just as we were taking our respective seats on the couch it occurred to me that I had seen this guy somewhere . . . *but where?* I couldn't pinpoint it. So I did what I usually do when I am unable to place a person, I stared at him for what felt like ages but it must have not been more than a few moments before I placed his face with a name. I had seen his picture or a picture of someone who looked very similar to him at the house I had just left my stuff in, took a shower in, and walked out of. Was Sid Mr Sharma's son? If yes, then that made him Tamanna's boss, the young and ambitious Mr Sharma who had climbed up the corporate ladder in record time and was very passionate about his job.

There was only one way to find out. 'Are you . . .?' I asked and paused at the word abruptly. 'No, we are not dating,' he said, laughing. The laugh was so smooth, he was so smooth, he made me look like a chimp in front of everyone and no, I was not asking him whether he was dating Adira. She had told me they were just friends and I believed her—this over-smart, overgroomed man need not tell me that. 'I was not asking you that because I know!' I gave him a curt smile while taking off my mask. The atmosphere in the room changed and he was not the happy guy any more. He looked at me with squinting eyes. He was the son of my new landlords, his pictures were all over their home, and I was planning to leech off his parents' niceness for the next two weeks. Was I happy about it? I had no time to think about it. First things first, was he who I thought he was? Because, if he was, that would mess up things a bit—for me, of course, as he was the hotshot single manager with wonderful parents.

'Do you work at Zantra Advertising with Tamanna?' I asked.

'What? You know my best friend?' Adira squeaked at the mere mention of Tamanna's name.

'I do know her. She is a part of the team that I lead,' he said emphasizing 'team I lead'. I heard it as he meant for her to hear it.

'What? And you are telling me now?' I loved to see Adira all hyped up and happy about things but not at that moment. It is easier said than done, you know, being happy for the one you love, but I was trying. I am not perfect, but I was trying to improve for her.

'I didn't mean to tell you even today about my work and you never told me that Tamanna is your best friend or we could have maybe tried to piece it all together.' Great! So I initiated the conversation and I was now out of it. She beamed at him and he twisted in his seat. She was making him blush. How much more romantic could it get for him? I wondered and cleared my throat. My tiny noise was met by glares from Adira's mother. I had completely forgotten that she was still there just as Sid and Adira had forgotten about my presence in the room.

Ignoring her eagle eye, I said, 'It was I who started the conversation really, because I am living in your house.' I shrugged as all eyes turned towards me. Sid burst into a big laugh and then asked, 'You what?'

'Did you have a word with Tamanna about a guy who was planning to live with you until he found a place to live? That is me,' I spelt it out for him, and he nodded as if mentally kicking himself to have agreed to keeping me with him.

'Oh Ronnie, that is so nice!' Adira looked between us and threw me a generous smile, the one that I feel is always reserved just for me, with her pearly set of teeth on display.

'Yes, it is,' Sid said, not meaning the words at all and I nodded, not taking my eyes off him. It was a strange situation. I was offered tea which I declined because I wanted to just be with Adira and not be slowly poisoned by her mother. So I did what I had come there for. I started talking to Adira about things that only we spoke about, such as my family, our friends, et cetera, but shameless Mr Sharma kept intruding into our conversation.

Adira had begun her physiotherapy again and was feeling much better. The limp was for life, but her legs hurt much less when she stood up for hours at a time or walked up and down the stairs. She needed fewer painkillers now, which was a piece of great news. She was excited to have Samba there and I told her all that there was to know about his schedule before Sid and I left her place in our cars. He drove a Creta but it didn't bother me much because, unlike her mother, Adira was so not into anything materialistic. But somewhere I did know that this guy stood a chance with her, he stood a chance with anyone that he was interested in. Once inside his house, his parents made me meet him and neither of us told them that we had met at Adira's house because he had not told his parents anything about his visits to her and they always thought that he was out for some work. I kept mum because I didn't know his parents' take on the situation as Adira's mother and Sid's mother were friends and I didn't want to make things awkward for me while I stayed at their home. They were all nice people honestly, including Sid, and barring him, they were being very nice to me too. There was no need for unnecessary friction.

Happiness is like a universal emotion. You are happy the same way as someone else is, the intensity may be different, but it's happiness nevertheless.
Sadness, however, hits everyone differently.

Adira

Life is funny and sometimes so damn confusing. So here I was, confused as to what I wanted. Sid and Ronnie were going to be living together for the next two weeks and they both came to see me every evening after office hours. I could feel the tension between the two guys but none of them said anything to me. Ronnie was desperate to move into his own space and I had spoken to Mummy asking if we could accommodate him. We lived in a big enough house and Samba was anyhow well-integrated, within three hours of moving in with us. He slept under Mummy's bed and was always snooping around the house, sniffing everything with his wet snub nose.

Seeing Ronnie still made my heart flutter and my pulse rate accelerate. Surely there was pain in the past, but there was also laughter, love, happiness in those moments that I could not stop revisiting. We had a history and judging by the looks in his broody eyes I knew that he thought that we had a future too. By the end of week one, I had realized one more thing, I did not want to meet both the boys together as Ronnie and I had things to talk about, things that I didn't want to discuss in front of Sid. He had been nice to me, he made me laugh, he wanted to know me more, he spoke less and was a good listener; of course, he was a good-looking man too, but he was not what my heart craved for. He was interested in me, I knew that, and he knew that I knew. So, I told him that he could find someone better. But my mother was more than interested in him being a part of my life and kept calling him over every time she came to know that Ronnie would be around. We couldn't go out because COVID was still around and by then we knew that it was here to stay. So, all we could do was meet up on the terrace after Ronnie's work and sometimes go for a walk in the park with our masks on.

Ronnie didn't like the idea of a walk despite that being the most time we spent alone, in each other's company. He did not like me putting 'undue' pressure on my legs. I understood his concern, but I was more interested in our time together at that stage than the pressure and being able to make any sense of what was going in me, what was going through my heart. I needed to spend some uninterrupted time with him. Every time I told him I was confused about my feelings, especially after he told me that he loved me, he went silent and after a long pause just said, 'I understand. I brought it all upon us. But I am going to give you as much time as you need.'

He was giving me time but what I needed was his time! I prayed more than him that he found a place to live. We needed to solve the puzzle of emotions that we were presented with, and we could do that together in that place. Ronnie was now a different man. I had seen him transform into this man who was committed to his idea of helping teachers. He was so passionate about his start-up; he had client meetings lined up and he was managing it all with his present job, staying away from his family while also making time for me. Just yesterday, when I was cribbing about the lack of something inspiring in my life, he proposed that I manage the client relations for his start-up. He couldn't pay me, like a job would do, which meant I would be working for free until some profits were made, and I was to be their fourth partner. I was more than thrilled at the prospect. We had worked together in the past, but it was for someone else. This opportunity was more than anything that I could ask for; it was like a dream. I did believe a lot in his start-up. So, I said yes!

My mind keeps telling me that I could have done more, should have done more.
But my heart tells me that I did what I could have and it is time for us to move on.
It is time to do what has to be done in the present moment and let go of the past.

Ronnie

While the first week living in Chandigarh was not bad, it was not very good either. I got to see Adira every day but in a controlled environment. Her mother or Sid were always with us, sometimes one of them was present in the room and sometimes both were. I wanted to talk to Adira now that she was opening up to me but we hardly got any chance to move on from the common topics as we were both aware of the lingering eyes and ears in the room. Most weekdays when both Sid and I worked, we spent the evenings at her home and the visits lasted for no more than half an hour. While I had the pretext of visiting Samba, Sid made no such attempt to hide the motive of his visits. He confidently stated time and again that he was there to meet both the women as he enjoyed their company a lot. Both mother and daughter were showered with equal amounts of compliments, ensuring that the older woman loved and adored him more than the daughter, and therefore was keen that he got a chance to woo her daughter and become a permanent addition to their family. Even in my presence on a few occasions, her mother had mentioned that she was worried that Adira was old enough to get married now.

With no hint of shame or nervousness, Sid had always responded that he was so much in love with them that he wanted the best for the family. I sometimes wondered whether he had also confessed his feelings towards Adira to her, if not in person, then definitely via her mother or over a text. But Adira never hinted that she knew, at least not in my presence. I was jealous, to say the least, but I could do nothing about it. She was not with me, she had a life and if she was looking for a life partner, she had every right to do so the same way I had every right to feel insecure and be grumpy about it. I was not being a child, no, I was way past that stage. But every time I saw the two of them in the same room, I wanted to kill my host's son.

However, I also knew that getting angry with Sid was not going to take me anywhere. In fact I was not upset with him, I was upset with myself for I had had the heart of the most beautiful girl god had made—I do not just mean physically. Adira has the most beautiful heart and soul. She was mine and I lost her; honestly, almost everyone lost her because of me. It was as if fate had placed the key to lifelong happiness in my palms and instead of holding on to the key tightly and keeping it secure, I let it slip through my fingers and break.

My mother says, '*Aap mare swarg ni milta*', which translates to 'one who wants to visit heaven has to die first'. I needed to work to get her back. She loved me once; I was the same person, so she could love me again. I knew forgiving me was also involved for her to come back to me, but I also knew that where there is love, forgiveness is bound to reside in that heart. She is a forgiving person; not that I wished to take advantage of that knowledge. Adira was not a person who held grudges and I hoped and prayed that one day she would find enough space and love in her heart to forgive me for my sins. Till then, I had to try and not sulk out in the open.

So, the first Saturday, I decided to make the evening special for her. Taking her out was not an option, so I decided to ask her for a virtual date night. She was to be in her house and I in the one that I was staying in, but we would still be alone as well as together. So, after she replied to my customary good morning message, I sent her another text to ask her if she was in and would like to watch an old Hindi movie on Netflix.

Me: I WAS WONDERING IF YOU WOULD LIKE A MOVIE DATE WITH ME

Adira: HA HA VERY FUNNY! THEATRES ARE CLOSED

Just as I had expected her to say.

Me: I MEAN A NETFLIX MOVIE DATE

Adira: I DIDN'T UNDERSTAND. YOU WANT TO WATCH A MOVIE HERE? AT NIGHT? MUMMY WILL KILL YOU!

I knew her mother's intentions very well and so did she.

Me: NO! I MEANT THAT WE COULD WATCH THE SAME MOVIE IN OUR RESPECTIVE ROOMS ON NETFLIX AT THE SAME TIME.

Adira: HOW IS THAT A DATE, DUMBO?

Me: BECAUSE WE WILL BE ON FACETIME, SO TECHNICALLY WE WILL BE WATCHING IT TOGETHER BUT VIRTUALLY.

It sounded like a crazy idea, but desperate times needed desperate measures, and this was my idea of a virtual date that I wanted to try. Thankfully, she agreed. She was not sure how well it would work but she didn't say it out loud. I could make that out when I spoke to her a few minutes later. She sounded confused but at my request, she agreed to give it a try.

I wasted the day mostly daydreaming and thinking of what I would say to her, how we would be on a video call for so long. My heart fluttered every time I thought that this would be our first date since the accident and that she had said yes after some cajoling, but she did say yes nevertheless. Finally, at nine sharp, I put a packet of popcorn in the microwave, picked up a bottle of Coke, and bolted the door of my room. Sid, who had been eyeing me suspiciously all the time, asked me what my plans were for the night as he planned on going out for a walk. I knew that meant he was going for a quick visit to Adira and I let him go alone for a change. We had been behaving like pre-teenagers for a while and it had to stop. So, unlike the other times when I deliberately stood at the door and made him go round and round in circles before he walked over to their home, I let him go without any drama and so he grew more suspicious. Sometimes, shamelessly, I even followed him to her house and made it a joint visit. Not that I am ashamed of it; okay, maybe a little ashamed, but shame takes you nowhere. However, that evening I did no such thing.

So, he sneaked out and I sneaked in. I texted Adira to check if she had decided the name of the movie we were watching. I had browsed Netflix and hadn't found a decent Hindi movie that I thought she would like so I outsourced the work to her. She was better at these things and it was no surprise that my phone pinged as soon as I was done typing. She wanted to watch *The Notebook*.

Me: WHAT? NOT A HINDI MOVIE?

I did not mind watching English movies as such but unlike a Hindi movie, an English movie requires a different level of concentration from me. I had to not just concentrate on the names and the faces so that I did not get confused, but I also had to keep an eye on the subtitles. Do not get me wrong; understanding English is not a challenge for me, but understanding the fast-paced, accented English in a Hollywood movie is a different ball game altogether. Suddenly, I felt my hands getting clammy and sweat appearing on my temples. But she had made a choice and I was not going to ask her to choose something else. So, *The Notebook* it was. Sid was still at her house, so I decided to do a quick search on Google and get a head start. I read the plot and realized that it was based on a book by the same name. I did not have enough time to go through anything related to the book, so I stuck to the Wiki page and clicked on the section around the plot. The plot grabbed my attention—two young lovers are separated because the mother doesn't think that the boy is suitable for her daughter. Before I could read half the plot, my phone's screen flashed with her face.

It was Adira. I quickly answered the call and the first words I heard were from Sid talking in the background. It had been more than fifteen minutes and he was still at their home. *Bastard*! I wanted to mutter but not while on a call with the girl who seldom cursed, so I waited for her to say hello, trying to calm my anger in the meantime.

'Hi, are you okay with the movie?' she asked me. *Was I?* I didn't know. I was not very happy about the fact that it was an English film, but I did want to know what happened next. I was intrigued, I wanted to know what happened to Noah and Allie's story.

'The story sounds interesting. I want to know how it ends,' I told her, adding that I had Googled the plot.

'What? You have not read the book yet?' she asked me as if I had told her that I had grown ten heads during the night. No, I had not read the book as I hardly read books. But she reads books, especially the ones about love and romance and I recalled that I had to send her a very special book for it was time that she read it. Before I could say anything more, her mother called her and she had to hang up with a promise to call back again in ten minutes. Five minutes later, I heard our main door open and Sid walked in. I fired up my laptop and attached my headset. Netflix came on and so did Adira's call. 'So how are we doing this?' she asked as soon as the call connected. She was wearing a pink night suit with a big collar that hid most of her neck. Her hair was in a braid on the side, and she had her specs on.

'When did this happen?' I asked, pointing towards her spectacles and she furrowed her eyebrows at me. 'They are for the screen, but I did have some eyesight issues due to the accident. I now have another pair for reading,' she told me. I felt so bad for even bringing it up that I went quiet. She sensed it.

'So, how are we doing this?' she asked me again, killing the silence. 'Where are your popcorn and Coke?' I asked her, picking up my movie essentials and dangling them in front of the screen. She held hers and we giggled like kids for a moment before she moved the camera away from her face towards her laptop, *The Notebook* was all set to begin there too.

'Okay, so now we can plug in the headsets and start watching the movie together and our calls can stay on speaker. Keep the phone somewhere where I can see you.' She did exactly as I told her. My plan was foolproof, but I had failed to notice that I was more than a fool. We were just five minutes into the movie when Adira's mother walked into her room. It looked as if she had not locked her room that evening or maybe she never did as she lived with her mother. I had assumed that she did. We paused the movie as her mother inquired what we were doing on a call with laptops in front of us. She had heard my not-so-subtle laughter on the speakerphone and assumed that

I had somehow managed to sneak into their home without her knowledge. Someone needed to tell her that I was not talented enough to sneak into her home virtually without her walking in, so how could she expect me to do a sneak attack in person?

Anyway, realizing that we were on a virtual date night and planned to watch a movie together, she invited herself over and our date of two became a party for three. I was not complaining much as I wanted Adira to be with me, and her mother and Adira were a kind of package deal now. So we resumed the movie. Adira's face flashed on my screen along with her mother's now and I still kept glancing at her. She was so absorbed in the movie that she didn't realize that she had picked a few pieces of popcorn in her hand that was mid-way to her open mouth for a while. Ideally, someone with an open mouth should look funny but not her. Her lips made an O and she was breathing lightly with her eyes fixed in concentration. She looked like the same girl I had seen years ago getting out of the auto in front of Nani's house. Before I could go back in time mentally, I felt her mother's eyes on me; she was looking at me. She was not angry, or upset or maybe she was, but I was so lost in the moment that I didn't notice it. But her gaze was a cue for me to switch my eyes back to the laptop screen. My ill fate was not going to end at the intrusion by her mother. There was more to come, and I didn't have to wait long before it did.

Adira's video paused a moment later. I wondered what happened and called her again. She disconnected and called me back after two minutes. It was a video call but with a twist. Sid was getting bored and wondered if he could join the movie. I wondered for how long he had been listening to us, standing outside my room, before he decided to barge into my date. When he could just watch the movie in his room, why did he have to be a part of our date was what I wanted to ask, but was it a date any more? Not really, so I opened the door of my room expecting him to be outside. He was there grinning away with his refreshments—a packet of chips and Fanta.

There was no point in looking at Adira and getting caught by her mother, so I moved all my concentration to the movie while Sid joked around with Adira's mother time and again. I blocked their conversation out as the movie about eternal love found its place. It was the most relatable and beautiful movie for us. Adira had chosen well. At every stage when the movie made our eyes water, we found ourselves staring back at each other. It was as if we were Noah and Ellie but in a different zone, in a different country. I could see her emotions floating into her tears; her mother felt it too. Finding that Noah and Ellie did grow old together filled me with love and hope. When I saw her mother squeeze her hand, I knew that she knew Adira loved me, just like I loved her. She was hurt but our love was greater than anything else in the world. The movie also made me understand that many things happen in life. A couple is tested by time, situations, people, loved ones, society, fate, and even their ego. What matters most is whether or not the love they have for each other wins every time they are faced with a test. Despite not being alone in a room, when the movie ended it felt that we were alone together and that no one mattered as much as we did. Despite being a constant chatterbox, Sid, too, wiped a few tears time and again and so did Adira's mother.

We bid each other good night on the call, and I kicked Sid out of my room. Despite seeing him cry, my feelings for him had not changed. I hated him for trying to take everything

away from me. We were rivals and there was no other way
about it. It was nearly midnight; I swept my bed clean with my
hands as I contemplated whether or not to text her. Then I did.

THANKS FOR THE MOVIE, I texted.

IT WAS SO BEAUTIFUL! she replied.

Yes! It was, I love you, I wanted to reply but typed: YES
instead and waited for her to say something more, anything.
I had said so much to her, confessed my love so many times in
the past, and asked for forgiveness, that it felt like a burden to
say those things again. I didn't want her to be upset with my
constant pleas; I wanted her to be happy and I wanted her to
be happy with me. So, after waiting for a while, I typed my last
message for the day: I HAVE A BOOK THAT YOU WOULD LIKE TO
READ . . . IT IS A LOVE STORY.

It seemed she had gone off to sleep because there was no
response, but I knew that we would meet in person tomorrow.
I had to give her the book that India had fallen in love with.

All stories have endings, all endings are new beginnings.
Not every ending is the end!

Ronnie

At the end of two weeks, I still had no place to live. With COVID not planning to go anywhere, it was tough to find a safe place within my budget. While Sid's parents had been nice to me and were willing to let me stay for a few more days, I knew that a few more days was not magically going to either increase my spending capacity or sprout affordable homes for me to choose from. I had found a new family while living with them. Sid's mother cooked me warm meals and his father liked spending time with me in the mornings as Sid liked to sleep late. Adira had more than once told Sid that she was not looking for anything beyond a platonic friendship and he seemed to have taken the hint. I knew that because I had seen him play around with his drone on the terrace on more than one occasion and the drone always returned with the phone number of a girl from the neighbourhood. His visits to Adira's house had also decreased drastically over the last few days. The best part was that he was now helping me with data on TeachMee. While we still had a lot of unanswered questions, he managed to sort the major issue—with his data backing us up, we had thirty-seven schools and fourteen independent universities backing us. While things were going great for us, I still did not wish to burden the family and overstay my welcome.

So, by the second Friday, I had made up my mind to leave Samba with Adira and her mother and go back to Delhi. It would be tough to leave them behind, all of them, including Adira's mother, at this stage. Times were tough and life is the most important thing for a human. With the deadly virus around us, every life was at stake. My parents, too, were worried about me, especially with the frequent moves to and from Delhi. Mummy warned me enough times not to take public transport or anything close to it at any cost. On the fourteenth day of my stay, I paid Adira and her mother a visit. The summer sun was not at all merciful and it was as hot as a desert. I wondered what had happened to the initial claims on TV about the COVID virus dying as soon as the weather became hot enough. Maybe it was not hot enough for the virus because it was clearly not going anywhere.

Reaching their house, I rang the bell and sanitized my hands. One can never be too careful with the coronavirus. Adira's mother came to open the door and I touched her feet. She, for a change, kept a feather-light hand on my shoulder as an acknowledgement. That was new.

'I wanted to see Samba and Adira before I go back to Delhi,' I informed her, as she stepped further into the house. I followed her looking around and calling out Samba's name. Not that I expected him to hear my voice and come running over. He had made his place in the house very clear when I was here the last time. The pug was seated under the table as Sid and I dined with the mother–daughter duo. I sat opposite

Adira to be able to see her all evening while Sid occupied the seat right next to her, whispering into her ear at every given opportunity as I burnt from within. Adira wore a yellow suit that evening and Samba sat between her and her mother on the floor, nibbling on Adira's dupatta. Never in my life had I thought I would say this but all during that evening, I wished to trade places with Samba as he curled up in her lap later and played with her dupatta.

I went further into the house and, as expected, found Samba lying in the living area where Adira sat on a couch with her feet up on the centre table. She was reading a book, a book that I had suggested to her. By the look of it, Adira was halfway through the book and was completely engrossed in it.

'Hi,' I said, to capture everyone's attention. Adira gave me a warm smile and I noticed that she had tied her hair with a scarf, a new habit of hers that suited her well. A few strands of hair fell on either side of her face. I noticed that her face looked fuller and her cheeks were flushed. She looked healthier than when I had come to Chandigarh a few days ago. I was so happy to see her that I completely forgot about everything else and opened my arms to hug her. She looked puzzled as she first looked at me and then behind me and that was when I realized that her mother was standing right behind me. But my arms were open, and I had to hug someone to lessen my embarrassment. I sat down and looked at Samba to save my honour and not make myself look like a fool. But Samba was determined not to let anything come between me and embarrassment. He lifted his head, looked at me, made a gruff sound, and went back to sleep. Adira chuckled and I heard her mother snort. In any other circumstance, I would have been really upset but Adira's chuckle made me look up at her. She was looking at Samba with her eyes wide and an infectious smile. I smiled along and shrugged, completely ignoring her mother.

Well, she didn't like it, of course, and made her displeasure known. 'He doesn't want to hug you either,' Adira's mother said, with the emphasis on the word 'either'.

I was instantly fuming at her words and felt my ears get warm. 'It's okay, this one is just lazy,' Adira said, getting down on the floor and patting Samba. We looked at each other and I felt the energy in the room change, I felt the spark. I couldn't take my eyes off her and going by the amount of time she held my gaze, neither could she. I could see her face flush and her pupils dilate. Just as I felt that she would say or do something, her mother cleared her throat and ruined the moment. Adira placed a palm on my shoulder and I helped her get up.

Just before we could have a chat, her mother got a phone call on her landline number, taking her to the room where she worked all day. Their living area had teal-coloured couches, a white centre table, and a white day bed. It was very well-lit and gave a resort-like vibe. I had never been invited to this part of the house as it was only meant for entertaining her mother's work clients or important guests. Sid, however, would have been here and sat on those couches, I could bet my kidneys on that. However, now, as Sid was out of the picture, I took him out of my mind. I sat on the day bed as she took a place on the couch.

'Sorry about her, I do not know what it will take for her to warm up to you,' she was indeed apologetic and her eyes conveyed the same. I felt so bad for her. It was not her fault that her mother and I didn't get along.

'It doesn't matter to me,' I shrugged as I confessed.

Her face fell instantly and she muttered in a very low voice, 'But it matters to me.'

That was the ray of hope that I had been waiting for and she had given it to me without her even realizing what she had done. She wanted me and her mother to get along because she cared for both of us and was torn between our constant cold war! I always knew that the mother–daughter duo was a package deal, Adira's mother had been with her when she needed her, her love was selfless and there were months when her mother had cared for her like a newborn child when she couldn't move after the accident. It was not fair for me to make her choose and it was not fair for her mother to make her choose either. Having said that, I also knew that the woman in question had gone through a lot in her own life and I had to try to make it better with her.

'I will try and win her over, for you,' I proclaimed. She patted Samba who was making himself comfortable under her feet again on the lush carpet. I couldn't see her face after I told her that I would try and mend my relationship with her mother, but I hoped that it gave her happiness and showed that I was pretty serious about our relationship and what I said. Adira had her loyalties in place and that was one of the things that I loved most about her.

'So,' I began. I had to tell her why I was there. I didn't want to leave this city, not at this time when we were finally getting somewhere but I had tried everything I could. 'I couldn't find a place,' I said.

She looked up and stared at my face waiting for me to complete what I wanted to say, and I continued, 'So, I will have to move back and I do not know how I will be able to come back to see you.' I didn't want to break down in front of her. But with everything that I had been through over the past few months, with Nani's passing and my parents being stuck in another country, I was in a very vulnerable space myself. While I tried to maintain that I was strong and emotionally together, the fact was that everything around me was collapsing and I was not blind enough to not see it. Adira and I were in a better space, but we were not where I wanted us to be. Going back and living alone in Delhi was going to be a nightmare but I had to do what I had to do. So, that evening was going to be a 'goodbye meeting' and we were to not meet each other for as long as it would take for COVID to leave us and things to get normal again.

'Did you ask the Sharmas to let you stay over for some more time?' she asked me a question I didn't want to answer. They would not say no but I was indebted already, and I could not take more from them.

'They need some family time,' is what I told Adira. She nodded in understanding. 'So will you be taking the fuzz basket with you?' She was referring to Samba, of course. Though my initial plan was to leave him with the women he adored much more than me, I was having second thoughts sitting there. Would I be able to live alone in the house without him? No matter how useless I felt he was around the house, he was a constant presence, a warm, fuzzy, perpetually hungry presence that helped me take my mind off things that kept me awake at night.

When I moved my head indicating a yes, she looked at him and gave him a tight hug. 'I do not think Mummy would like that,' she stated the obvious. I had seen her mother talk to Samba more often than she had ever spoken to me. She took him out for walks every morning and evening and fed him by hand when he was fussy. I just sighed and nodded in response. Of course, she was going to miss him.

'Who is taking whom?' Her mother stomped into the room as if on cue to make the conversation more awkward. I looked at the older woman and saw how difficult it would be to let the dog go. At that stage, I didn't know that the said dog was going to change my life for the better.

'Ronnie has to go as the Sharmas need more space in the house and he couldn't find a house in his budget; he is also taking Samba back to Delhi,' her daughter informed her and I observed the older woman's eyes go twice their size. She was not expecting this. She looked at the animal in question and walked over to sit next to Adira.

'What is your budget?' she asked me the embarrassing question. Honestly, I did earn enough to support myself but I was not a manager like Sid or a businessperson like Adira's mother. I had a future to think about and I was saving for that future. I saved a lot, which meant mercilessly cutting my budgets. But I had to tell her the ballpark amount that I had in mind so that she could help if that was her intention.

'Fifteen thousand with food and bills,' I told her honestly.

'You cannot find an independent place in that amount. See, I am not belittling you, but Chandigarh is an expensive place.' She didn't need to tell me that. I had been house-hunting for the past several days and knew that already.

'Why won't the Sharmas keep you?' The same question, a different person, and I gave her the same response. They need more family space, a lie, but it made things less awkward. 'Okay, but you can't take him,' Adira's mother stated, as if Samba was her dog and then realized that she had been a little out of line to say it that way, so she turned around and added a suggestion, 'You can stay here.'

That statement sounded so unreal, I felt the earth move and I am not even exaggerating. I knew that it could have been the heat of the moment, but I was not letting the opportunity slide.

Rewinding the clock doesn't reverse time but sometimes, life gives us a second chance just so that we can do things over again.

Let us start over again
Let You and I be strangers again
Let me make a space for myself in your heart again
Let me make you laugh again
Let us unlearn what we know about each other again
Let us make new memories and give each other a chance again

Ronnie

I did not waste any time in taking up the offer and moved in with Adira and her mother the same night. My bags were already packed as I had plans to move back, so exactly half an hour after I was given the option to move in, I did so. The first thing that I did after moving into their home was to hand over 15,000 rupees to the landlady, fondly known as Adira's mother.

While I had more than a few dreams related to being close to Adira, they came crashing down as soon as I got to know that I had been assigned a room close to her mother's. I knew the reason why she still didn't trust me enough. It was like the saying, 'Keep your friends close and your enemies closer'. Samba was the friend, and I was not. So, I was as careful as possible, ensuring that I never lingered around too long near her daughter's room when she was alone in there. We usually sat and talked in the living area and that too mostly when her mother was around us. The only two times when we were on our own during the day were when her mother went out with Samba for his walks. I had asked her if she wanted me to do that, but she insisted on taking him out on her own.

She trusted me around Adira for those fifteen minutes and I never abused that trust. Mostly when she came back home, she found us sitting on the terrace or in her study chatting about general stuff. By the third day, her mother had warmed up to me a little and had started asking me what food I would like, which was comforting as I was away from my mother. My customary calls to my parents every evening lasted longer nowadays because Adira always wanted to see my niece and talk to my sister and mother while Papa and I looked at the ladies and wondered how much they had to talk about!

Honestly, I was extremely happy with the way things were turning out with Adira's mother warming up to me and maybe even the idea of 'us'. Okay, I agree that the thought of us was not that welcome yet, but my parents were over the moon. Sometimes the two mothers too chatted a bit; they had less in common which meant there was always a scarcity of topics of conversation. It was mostly the usual pleasantries followed by, '*Aur sab theek*?' (Is everything else okay?) And that was that. From the day I moved in, Sid became a visitor in the house while I lived in there and he naturally understood that Adira and I went a long way back. His intrusion in my life was minimal as he limited his visits now, not that I was complaining about anything. Adira had taken up her job as the client manager in our venture very seriously and was in talks about a meeting with the clients soon for a 10 million dollar funding approval. Sid's visits were mostly related to him helping her out with the project. Incidentally, he had made more female friends and had to make visits to their homes, too, so usually he had limited time.

Speaking of friends, Tamanna and Piyush called regularly every week and gave me an update on their baby. I knew that

Tamanna spoke to Adira more often than Piyush spoke to me and they always exchanged pictures of her namesake. Adira always forwarded them to me. Those were the only messages that I got on my phone from her since I had moved in as their paying guest. It was obviously because we were living under the same roof, and we could talk about anything that we wanted to in person. Having said that, I also learnt that it was not very easy to talk about everything in person, especially if the things that one needs to talk about are matters pertaining to the heart. One more reason why I wanted her and me to interact with each other over texts and WhatsApp a little more was because it was so easy to revisit the conversations in texts. I did that every night before I slept. It was an old habit that sounds crazy but is very soothing. I scrolled through our chats before sleeping and smiled like a lunatic remembering something or the other. But now all I had to scroll through were a lot of baby pictures and our customary good morning messages. I still sent those and she usually responded with an emoticon.

On the first Saturday after I moved in, I was in for a surprise. As much as I want to tell you that the surprise was from Adira, that was not the case. The surprise came from her mother instead. At around five in the evening, she called me to her study and asked me if I wanted to watch a movie.

'With you?' I was puzzled and she gave me an 'Are you out of your mind?' look.

'I mean the two of you. I know we intruded the other night.' So she knew what she was doing and still did it! I was not amazed by the truth but was amazed by her confession.

'Yes, I mean if she wants to watch a movie, then it's a definite yes!' I was squealing with happiness. How often does the mother of the girl you love ask you if you want to take her daughter out for a date? Technically, we would still be inside the house as going out was not an option then, but she was still arranging it for me.

'Great! I will ask her then,' she said and then quickly changed her mind. 'Or you can ask her. I will be gone for a couple of hours today and I would rather have you guys watch a movie than do something else,' she said, looking at me with one raised eyebrow and channelling her inner Nanny McPhee. *What exactly did she think I was planning to do with her daughter when she was out of the house?* I wondered how shallow a person she thought I was or how weak did she think her daughter was? I could vouch my life for the fact that no one, I mean no one in the world, could make her daughter do things that she didn't want to do, and she definitely didn't want to do 'those' things with me then. The things that her mother thought I was after, what I was looking for like the rabid animal she believed I was. I loved her and cared for her but that didn't mean I thought of just having sex at the first opportunity with her. I mean I did think of it but not all the time and never in her mother's house in the bed that she had had since she was a kid. Nah, that doesn't float my boat!

'I would ask her for sure, but I would first want to assure you that I have no intentions of doing whatever you thought I was going to do in this house,' I replied. The new courage could have cost me my new place; she was also my landlady, after all.

However, she didn't react; it was as if she'd not even heard me and resumed her paperwork. Her study was full of papers and I wondered if she was really making money out of her business or just spending all the money on printouts. She had, with her silence, dismissed me like a good-for-nothing butler but I still stood there. I had been itching to ask her a question and my stupid self believed that the only time that she had been nice to me was the right time to ruin it all! So I waited until she glanced up from the pile of paperwork again to look me in the eye. 'Did you ask Sid to come and join me that day when we watched the movie?' Her eyebrows shot up and I knew that I had asked the wrong question, but the words had been spoken, the question had been asked and she had to answer it.

'Why would I do that?' she asked the counter-question. I was expecting it and knew that any answer was bound to make the situation worse.

I contemplated fleeing but where was I to go? I lived in her house. So, I decided to be honest. 'Because he is better for Adira and you are friends with his mother.'

'See, Ronnie, I do not like you a lot.' Great! Thankfully she had more to add and I hoped that no more insults were coming my way, fingers crossed behind my back and prayers shooting up to the sky to every deity that I knew of. 'But I know that you are right for her. I have seen the way you looked after her when I took a break from taking care of her in the hospital. Despite no hope of her complete recovery, you never left her side, visited her even when I told you not to, came over to Chandigarh leaving everything behind, and now are staying with us when I have not been the best of hosts. I am not blind. I see everything and understand love and care. I will not lie to you, Sid is a great guy and he likes her too. His mother is a good friend, and nothing will please me more than if he is a part of Adira's life, but it is Adira's life and not mine. I know I cannot force love on her. While I know that she is not completely sure of you yet, I also know that you are the one who will open her heart again. She is in a space where she needs time and you have been giving her that.'

I could feel my cheeks burn now. Was she telling me all this or was I dreaming? I pinched myself a tad too hard and it hurt like hell. She was indeed there in person telling me all those things; now I could die in peace. I exhaled deeply and that was when she crushed my heart by saying, 'I will not lie if I tell you that you are the best person for her, but you are the right person for her and sometimes being the best doesn't matter. I know you cannot give her the life that I want for her where she doesn't have to worry about money and the material things that one wants. But I know that you and she can make a life that has everything you need to make it beautiful and I have made my peace with that.' So I was not the perfect choice according to her but I was perfect for Adira. I felt dizzy; she had a very complicated way of complimenting a person.

'So you didn't call Sid that evening, right?' I asked her like a fool, and she just shrugged as if telling me, 'You never know.'

This woman was very complicated, and I now knew where Adira got it all from. But, like a fool, I wished that both the mother as well as the daughter would be a part of my life for life. I left the room grinning from ear to ear, and knocked on Adira's door.

'It's open, Ma,' she said, assuming it was her mother, so I told her that it was me. A few moments later, she opened the door a bit. It was ten in the morning and she was still in her PJs. Instantly, I was worried about her health as she never stayed in her nightclothes past eight and was very particular about it.

'Are you okay?' I asked, looking at her flushed cheeks. She looked as if she had a fever or something so my hand instantly touched her forehead. Her temperature appeared to be in the normal range, at least upon touching.

'I am fine, was just playing with Samba,' she said and gestured behind her. Her bed was a war zone; Samba lay there spent as if he had run a marathon under the sheets. His soft toys were all over the place.

'Really?' I asked the dog. He had been getting naughtier by the day since coming to this house. He liked all the attention he got, and I wondered if he would ever want to leave with me.

Adira moved a little to give me some space and I walked into the room, our hands brushed ever so slightly and I felt goosebumps appear all over me. My body was behaving as if I was a teenager and I didn't like it. I inhaled her scent as she walked past the place where I stood and hopped on to her bed. She still smelled the same, of her favourite perfume, British Rose. To me, she smelled like home. This was the first time I had stepped into the room in a while so, like a curious cat, I looked around as she flopped on her bed, slumping a little more than usual. Must have gotten hurt while wrestling the pooch. 'Did you hurt your leg again?' I asked her, eyeing the dog who was now shamelessly on his back giving her access to his tummy which she was happily rubbing for him.

'Nah, just a light sprain,' she said, following my vision. I was looking at the pair of white teddy bears that she had got for me after the accident. I saw her hang her head a little and let out a small sigh before she looked up and met my eyes. The energy in the room shifted and I knew that I was not the only one feeling it. It took me a couple of seconds to come out of the maze that her eyes were; I was almost lost in there for eternity. What was I here to talk to her about? I wondered and squinted my eyes trying to recall. She mirrored my expression and looked so cute that I wanted to tell her the same and see her blush. But I didn't; I never do the right thing at the right time, and it turns out that this is the only thing that I am extremely good at! After a nanosecond, the fog in my brain cleared and I recalled I had to ask her about the movie.

'Your mother is planning to go somewhere this evening. I was wondering if you would like to watch a movie with me?' I asked her. She looked puzzled. 'I mean, she is going out and asked me if you and I would like to watch a movie together, so I told her that I would ask you. I mean, I . . .' I was rambling trying to explain.

'Yes,' she said softly. I stopped talking. We had been out countless times; been to movie theatres and watched dozens of movies while we were together. And yet, asking her for a movie that we planned to watch inside the house made me giddier, it made me more nervous and her 'yes' made me feel things in the pit of my stomach as if I were a teenager talking to my crush. The feeling was so funny that I loved it. She was looking straight at me.

'Okay! Great,' I said and turned on my heel. I had to check if we had enough popcorn and chips in the pantry. Then I stopped. 'Which movie?' I asked, realizing that we had only a few options on YouTube, Netflix and Amazon Prime. 'The same one, *The Notebook*,' she said.

I felt my throat tighten, I had cried so many times after watching that movie and even ended up reading the book because of the nostalgia and emotions the film gave me. I was not sure if watching the same movie with her was a very good idea. 'The same? Why?' I could not help but wonder out loud.

I saw her face fall and she looked like a lost child. 'We were going to watch it together the last time and couldn't. Also, it is one of my favourite movies,' she shrugged. I am an ass disguised as a human.

'I want to watch it again. I read the book, too, because I liked the movie so much,' I told her honestly and her face changed. So, it was decided, we were re-watching *The Notebook*. I couldn't wipe the crazy wide grin off my face as I looked around the kitchen to prepare a snack box.

At around four in the evening, I heard her mother getting ready. While she took her time, I was a bundle of nerves, a mixed bag of nervousness, excitement, love, longing, with a hint of anticipation.

As I saw Adira's mother walk out of her study all ready to head out with her mask on her face, I decided to tap on Adira's door to let her know that we were all set for the evening. My hands were exceptionally clammy so I stopped at the door to wipe them on my sweatpants when I heard her. Adira was humming. She sings only when she is happy and she was happy that evening. The thought gave me so much comfort that I have no words to describe what I felt. It was a gush of emotions and they were everything a person needs to feel as if they are flying. I pressed my ear to the door to figure out the song. I knew it had to be a Hindi song from the black and white era.

I have great luck with bad luck. As soon as my ear touched the door, a pat came on my left shoulder. We were just the three of us living in the house as even the house help was not there due to COVID. Earlier, her mother used to do all the housework but ever since I had moved in, I was the unofficial maid. Not that I was complaining; her mother is an excellent cook and a little work around the house in exchange for such amazing free food was a good deal, to be honest.

Coming back to the pat on my shoulder, I knew who it was before I even turned around. The hand belonged to the lady who cooked wonderful meals for me even though she didn't like me much. I turned around to face her, feeling all my blood rushing towards my face and changing my colour to beet. 'What do you think you are doing?' she asked, with her eyes wider than I have ever seen. I could not just make up an excuse right there and then as most of my brain cells froze up when this woman was around me. 'She is singing,' I told her very gently, not making a noise loud enough to be heard by Adira on the other side of the door. Her mother squinted at me and that was my cue to lower my gaze and leave before I made her change her mind about letting both of us watch a movie alone in the house.

Just before entering my room, I turned around to see if Adira's mother was still giving me death glares when I saw the most beautiful sight. Adira's mother stood at the same spot where I was standing earlier with her ear glued to the door and she had a smile on her lips. She too knew what her singing meant; her daughter was happy.

Sometimes she is too much of everything—too sensitive,
too generous, too intense, too adorable, too accepting. She is mad,
the kind of mad that makes you fall in love and she doesn't need
much—some books to read, a warm touch, someone to love and
to be loved.

Adira

I chose the movie, he got us snacks and just like that in the living room, we had our movie date. It was a new feeling to be with him all alone in the house, that too with my mother's permission. I wanted to ask Mummy why but decided against it. She was willing to meet me halfway and I appreciated that. Any random and uncalled-for interrogation would have just spoiled everything and that was the last thing I wanted.

At around five in the evening, Mummy went over to a friend's house. They had a big garden and they planned to do a get-together with all the social distancing protocols in place. She kissed me goodbye and told me to enjoy the movie before going out. I closed the door behind her and Ronnie called out, 'Has she gone?' from his room.

'Can you be a little quiet?' I shouted back. 'She must be just around the corner right now!' When he peeped out, I was amazed at how happy his face looked because my mother had left the house. *Just how much did these two hate each other?*

'She has gone, where is Samba?' I asked him. I had not seen that guy since he left my bedroom in the afternoon.

Ronnie walked out of his room with Samba in his arms, 'This one? He just found out where his loyalties should lie. He loves me the most,' he tried to tease me as Samba wriggled in his hold.

'Ha ha, I know that we both know that Samba loves me more and he loves my mother the most,' I told him, looking at his struggle to contain the dog in his embrace.

'Whatever! We are waiting for you in the guest room,' he said and turned on his heel to enter his room or as he called it, the 'guest room'.

'But I thought that we were watching it on the TV here,' I said and followed him into the room. It was the first time I had entered the room since he had moved in and, to my surprise, it was very neat and clean. The single bed was made and on it was a laptop bed table. The side tables had been moved a little to align them with the laptop and were stacked with cola and snacks. He flicked the lights off and switched on the LED strip under the bed. Blue light slowly filled the room, making it dimly lit, yet there was enough light to allow us to see each other's faces.

'Not bad,' I told him, patting his shoulder as I passed him and took a seat on the bed, propping my legs up and adjusting the cushions behind me. Samba followed me and I picked him up to make him sit next to me. Ronnie occupied the leftover space and a giggle escaped my mouth. He had made the place very cozy as well as beautiful for a date indoors. The movie started and we got lost in it, munching our way through some scenes and going back and forth in time. Our bodies relaxed and slowly our shoulders were touching and our feet were intertwined to make space for Samba who had dozed off.

As the movie ended, so did the trance that we were in and we took in our surroundings. Mummy was not yet home and my head lay on Ronnie's shoulder as I wiped my tears away.

'I forgive you for all that you did, you said, and for everything else that you did not do but blame yourself for,' I told him in a low voice.

'I know forgiving me would not have been easy after . . .' he left the sentence unfinished.

'But I forgive you for I believe that what we had and what we have is bigger than everything. I have seen you for the past several months, the way you have been trying to win me over. No one else would have done that for me,' I told him earnestly and raised my head to meet his gaze.

Ronnie

I blinked my eyes, unable to comprehend what she had just said. Did she say that she forgave me? So easily? I had hardly done anything to be worthy of her forgiveness. I was just in her life, waiting for her to forgive me without doing much and she, with her big heart, listened to my silent pleas and gave me just that—forgiveness!

I let out a sigh, not on purpose but it just came out of me as if something heavy was trapped in me; it was weighing me down and I was now lighter by several pounds. She raised her eyes to meet mine and I could see that she meant what she said even when she told me that what we have 'is bigger than all that we have gone through', all that she had gone through, and all I had been a part of. We had immense love in our hearts for each other which was more than what I had ever imagined was needed to be with a person for life. And yet, we were not together.

With some people, you do not need to say anything; they understand each movement of yours, they get to know everything you want just by looking into your eyes. Adira is that person for me, she knows me more than

I know myself, she understands me better than anyone else. Her eyes tell me that she had seen me suffer as she struggled to recover over the last several months. Her gaze told me that, despite my shortcomings, she knew that I loved her like no one else loved anyone. A fraction of what we have is enough to last other people for a lifetime, such is our love.

'Thank you,' I told her and rubbed my palms over my eyes, a habit I had recently developed to hide my nervousness or anxiety. Honestly, I had never thought that this moment would come again in my life, but it did and now that we were talking about 'us' again, I was at a loss for words. My tongue felt as if a stone had been tied to it; I was overwhelmed, to say the least. As I rubbed my palms over my face and felt her lightly touch the back of my hands with her soft palms, I lowered my hands to uncover my face. I could not cower at this stage. It was all that I had hoped, prayed, and asked for and I had to ensure that she knew it.

I opened my eyes and she smiled and leaned into me. Our faces were so close that I could see the pupils in her eyes dilate. She blushed as I moved my gaze to her lips and we kissed. It lasted a moment or maybe several; I was too lost in the moment to keep count. My head was buzzing with thoughts and feelings; there was no reasoning, no concept of time and space. All I could feel was her. My heart swelled with anticipation of a future and my fingers shook as I cupped her face thinking of how beautiful she was inside as well as outside.

In a very low tone, between the kisses, I repeatedly said 'I love you' to her and tears rolled down her cheeks as she said the words back. We are made for each other and anyone who thinks or tells me otherwise has no understanding of what love is.

Suddenly, one of the few people who love telling me otherwise, unlocked the main door and both of us sprang back to our sides of the bed. Adira's mother was back, just at the right time to spoil everything. But I could not complain as, after all, it was her idea that both of us should watch a movie and she gave us space too. So, no matter how much I wanted to hate her, I could not. After all, we were now stuck with each other for life, for I was not going to let these women walk away from me.

Adira swiftly left the room and Samba followed her, pausing many times on the way to stretch his tiny legs. I closed the door and lay on the bed, unable to move or think. I slept in the sitting position and woke up sometime after midnight realizing that I had not had any dinner. But my body ached and my throat felt as if I had swallowed a cactus. I adjusted myself in the bed and covered myself with a sheet. I was feeling very cold too. As I was trying to make some more space for myself, trying to move the laptop, it hit me—I was unwell and had signs of a cold. Was it COVID? I had been out of the house to get chips and Coke just before we watched the movie.

I was sweating with the realization; maybe I did have COVID. I had to get tested first thing in the morning and then isolate as per the guidelines if I was positive. I knew that the rate of recovery was high, especially for young people. The fact that there was no cure for it gave me chills. I decided to self-isolate and not step out of the room until the results came. I had missed my parents' regular video call that night and made a mental note to not tell them and give them an unnecessary scare.

'I need not tell Adira and her mother, too, until I get a confirmation,' I told myself when I realized that COVID was highly contagious and if I had been carrying it since the time I had come back from the shops, then I would have to tell Adira because, well, because we kissed and there was a very high chance that I had given her the deadly virus.

'Stay away from her and do not try any hanky-panky,' her mother's threat came back to me as if she was uttering those words just then in my ears. She would kill me. I had better start writing a will to transfer my assets to Adira as her mother would not give me a chance to do the same later. My life was over and there was no escaping the inevitable. I had to tell them in the morning, for their own good.

Just as I was about to sleep, there was a ping on my phone. It was a business email. I looked at it trying to make sense of what I was reading. The email carried that most awaited bit of news: a meeting with investors was scheduled in a week's time.

Who says there is no bad time for good news? It did not appear to be a great time for me to be able to make anyone invest in anything. While pondering over my relationship with luck, my eyes closed, and I went into a dreamless sleep.

With infatuation comes impatience.
With love comes serenity.

Ronnie

I was feeling very low the next morning and I did not need a doctor to confirm that I had caught some bug. I hoped it was not COVID but there was only one way to tell, I had to get to a testing centre and get myself checked. As contagious as the virus was, I didn't want to come in close contact with anyone and risk their health. It suddenly dawned on me that I had to tell Adira to get tested too. It was going to be a difficult task as we had kissed last night—it could have been the last kiss of my life! I hoped that she was okay and had not caught whatever I was living with. I was tempted to text or call her but then decided not to. If she too was unwell, it was better for her to rest. Even though I had been up since five in the morning due to a severe body ache and cold. Also, I recalled that sometime at night I had also managed to drop a text to my parents and then went off to sleep again. I had some twenty frantic phone calls from different numbers on my phone.

I had to call them back but first, I had to get tested. I had not even stepped out of my room yet and was waiting to hear some commotion from outside the room. Adira's mother was in the kitchen. I had to tell her, so I made a phone call on the landline which she didn't answer. I tried her cellphone too but as usual, it was on silent. Her mother picked up her phone only after nine-thirty every morning, which was a good practice and kept her away from unnecessary scrolling, something that I was addicted to these days. I had to go out and tell her in person, so I sanitized my hands and wore a fresh mask over my nose and chin. As soon as I opened the door, she turned around to face me. She had a smile on her face and looked happy that morning. Her face went from happy to worried in an instant and she asked me what happened.

'I am down with something, it could be COVID,' I told her blankly as there was no other way to say it.

'Oh,' escaped her mouth and her expression changed from worry to amusement. 'I do not think it is COVID, you are an attention seeker,' she said, giggling. 'Not every sneeze is because of COVID.'

'As much as I would be relieved to know that it is not, we cannot say just now that it isn't. I went out yesterday to get some chips from the local shop. I am going to get tested,' I informed the lady.

'Okay, get tested and stay in the room,' she told me, adding sternly, 'I will get you breakfast in bed.' I mean, offering me breakfast in bed was very kind and I didn't want to break what we had built, but I had to. So I told her that Adira should get tested too. I expected her to ask me why and then I had to tell her all about the kiss, making it a very awkward last conversation of my life before she murdered me with a kitchen knife. But she just nodded and said, 'All three of us will have to get tested and I will have to tell all the ladies I met last evening to isolate too until we get tested. I have been watching a lot of news lately. Telling all our close contacts to isolate is the best way to go about it.' She was being Miss Know-It-All and it worked in my favour for a change. I was expecting a different scenario to play out than the one I had just witnessed and so I was relieved.

'Yes!' I told her, silently thanking my stars, for luck was not always on my side. Her lack of interrogation meant that I was going to live to see another day. I asked her to check on Adira before I picked up the car keys and left to take a test alone. Adira and her mother were to go for a test together later that day.

Upon returning, I was relieved to know that Adira was not feeling any different and most likely had not caught the virus. I went immediately into my room where a hot breakfast awaited me at the door. I bolted my door from within, had a little food and took another nap. I woke up at around mid-day with a heavy chest and leaky nose. There were several messages from my loved ones making me feel good and bad at the same time. Indeed, I had a life full of love and I had been a fool to not have realized it earlier. I responded to everyone in one line that I copied and pasted across all chats: I am better now, yet to get the results.

There were many texts from Adira, too, asking me if I needed anything, and so on. Adira and I texted a lot that day. Around mid-day, Adira and her mother too got their tests done and we had to wait for twenty-four hours before the results came in. I kept having the Crocin and soups that her mother was preparing for me every few hours and leaving outside the door.

My parents called me at around seven in the evening. It was a video call like every day but I was a mess when I answered the phone. My mother started crying looking at me and then her crying became more intense when I told her that I had taken the test for COVID. She had been living in the UK and had seen the worst with people dying in crazy numbers. Papa was better, and did most of the talking. I told them about everyone's self-isolation. 'Does anyone else have any symptoms?' Papa inquired and I told him the truth. 'I am the only lucky one,' I tried to make a small joke which didn't go well with Mummy. She got angry and started counting all the stupid things I had ever done in my life since the beginning and how it had always been my fault. She was high on emotion, and I was high on cough and cold medicines, so I just closed my eyes and reached my happy place. Adira's face appeared, the wind playing with her hair, soft sand underneath her feet.

'Are you even listening to me?' My mother jolted me with her words. I had to open my eyes to face her, virtually.

'Adira's mom has been taking care of me, Mummy. She made me a lot of soup and got me medicines,' I told her in an attempt to reassure her. But the thing with Indian mothers is that they fear losing their children to other people, for instance, their spouses and their parents.

So she began, 'She is a career woman, she cannot nurse you back to health. You need your own mother, and I am stuck here. I do not know what wrongs I have done to see the day where someone else has to care for my unwell child . . .' Papa giggled sitting next to her and I could not stifle my laughter any more; no matter how much it hurt, I had to laugh and then cough and then laugh again.

The call lasted one hour and thirty minutes where I saw my niece and nephew, spoke to my sister and brother-in-law, and updated them on the situation in India as they filled me with anything and everything they knew about recovering from COVID. Even though it was not confirmed that I was coronavirus-positive then, my family had kind of declared that I was on my deathbed. I wondered what would happen if the test indeed came out positive.

The twenty-four hours till we got the results were the longest twenty-four hours of my life. While I was not going out of the room, Adira was, and every time she was around my room or I heard her stepping into the kitchen, I wanted to follow her, talk to her in person, and see her. We had not been in the same room since our disrupted kiss last night and it bothered me as I wanted to know what she felt about it, if she felt anything at all, and if she was sure of what she had told me. But nothing lasts forever; the twenty-four hours until the test result did pass like a kidney stone but they passed nevertheless. Thankfully, both Adira and her mother came out negative; however, I was COVID-positive. I had to self-isolate and take precautions but as I had symptoms mimicking the common cold, I didn't think it would be much of a deal at that time. Adira's mother prepared soups and kadhas (herbal cold concoctions) for me and I knew that I would be in perfect health in no time. The kadhas were my mother's recipes which she kept forwarding to Adira's mother. All my meals were left at my door to maintain isolation. I had still insisted that Adira should get tested again in three days because we had spent some alone time together and I was worried for her. Her mother had the same thoughts as mine and Adira agreed to take another test 'if needed'. Our meeting with the investors was in a week's time and I assumed that the cold would make me stick to my bed ensuring that I focused solely on the meeting and worked hard to secure the funding but, boy, was I wrong!

The most beautiful chapters in our lives are based on uncertainty.
Embrace love, embrace people, embrace what life offers.

Ronnie

Coronavirus was not just a mildly symptomatic flu for me. By the end of day five, I was tired the way I had never been tired in my whole life. My sense of smell and taste had vanished long ago, and my joints hurt as if I had been in an accident. There were no special medicines to be taken, I wheezed a lot and had difficulty concentrating. While it was difficult for me to breathe in certain positions at certain times of the day, it was weakness and pain that were killing me. The meeting was one day away and I was in no position to attend it. I was regretting my decision not to involve someone who was able to handle client meetings. Someone like Adira, but I could not ask her to just go to the meeting alone; she had never done this kind of work before and it would have been too much to ask of her. She had been helping me as much as she could. But I also knew in my heart that it was the best time for the app to be launched with so many students struggling and so many teachers who could use some extra income in these tough times. While I lay in bed doing some cost analysis for students as well as institutions, I heard a knock on the door. The door was already open. I looked up and saw Adira standing there, dressed in a peach sundress with a bowl of what I assumed was soup in her hand. I quickly slapped a mask on my face. 'Please do not come inside, leave it at the door and I shall pick it up,' I told her calmly, as if talking to a child.

She laughed at me and told me the same thing, 'Why are you talking to me as if I am a toddler? I am not the one who is unwell, you are.' She was right but I had lost Nani to COVID already, and I would never be able to bear it if I was the cause of Adira catching the deadly virus. I was worried for her and also for myself. If she did catch it, I would be in a worse mental state than I was in at that moment.

'Relax, will you?' she said, quirking an eyebrow when I didn't say anything, as if she was reading my mind. Normally I found her breezy attitude cute but at that moment, my anger took over me. I had nearly lost her once; she was still on medication. I saw a look of pity for me flood her eyes; I was okay with that. I was okay with everything as long as she was healthy. She kept the food at the door, dragged a chair in, and placed it at a little distance from the door. She could see me from where she sat and I her. While I carefully got off the bed, sanitized my hands and walked over to pick up the food, she untied her hair tie and let her long hair loose over her shoulders. Several strands fell on her face, and she tucked them behind her ears. I could tell that she had just taken a shower; her hair was not dripping wet but was not completely dry yet. She tilted her head a little, studying me as I walked over to pick up my plate.

'Why are you extra jumpy today? What is the matter?' While a lot had changed between us over the months, her ability to read me amazed me. I shook my head at the wonderful girl who sat right in front of me when I had told her to go back to her room more than once.

'The meeting is tomorrow,' I told her flatly. There was no reason to cover it up any more; I just wanted to hide it for as long as I could so as to not pass on my worries to her.

'With the big investors? From New York?' she asked me with her eyes wide in amazement, happiness brimming on her face.

It was a dream for me and she knew how much I wanted this dream to come true, almost as much as I wanted her to come back to me. This could make my career as an entrepreneur, this deal could be my first step into the world where I could achieve everything I wanted for myself and give Adira the promise of the life that she deserved. 'Yes, but my head is so heavy, and I feel like the worst symptoms of corona have hit me today. I tried to look at the presentation but couldn't concentrate at all. The screen made my eyes teary and . . .'

'I can go on the call for you,' she offered. 'I know about the project and the latest developments. I can handle it, trust me. I even spoke to the vendor who did the dummy video the other day, remember?' It was a fact, Adira and I had worked together over the last several weeks. She had been very keen to know about everything and I was more than happy to share the details. She knew more about the project than anyone else who had worked on it, including Piyush, but was she ready to take on such a big responsibility? The meeting was a make-or-break point for us.

'Will you be able to manage?' I didn't want to burden her with more work than she could handle. She raised one eyebrow asking me why I was questioning her ability. I was honestly not doing that; she was capable, but I didn't want her to overwork. Also, it had been my dream. I had been a part of everything related to TeachMee right from its conception and

I wanted to be a part of everything related to it in the future too. But I also knew that my condition was deteriorating and I was not in the right frame of mind to manage the call and bag the investment either. I had to think of the bigger picture, so I said yes and saw her jump and squeal in joy.

'I had been waiting for something like this, something that would make me get up and work! I will not disappoint you, trust me,' she said, nearly at the door now. I had a sudden urge to hug her and feel the warmth of her joy but that was not the right thing to do. So I just curled my fists and looked down at my plate; there was khichdi for me to eat.

'You eat in peace,' she said, 'and I will come back to you in some time so that we can prepare.'

I nodded and she ran back to her room.

We decided to sit together a few times that day for a knowledge transfer, virtually, of course. She knew most of the things and surprised me with her knowledge of the numbers and statistics that I had used for cost as well as profit projections. By the end of that evening, I was very confident of her as well as TeachMee. 'We are going to do great!' I told her at the end of the video call. She nodded at me, then her eyes squinted at the screen. She was still looking at the slides and seemed to be thinking about something.

'What happened?' I asked.

'The initial projections in the first two slides were revised by you three weeks ago,' she told me, and I moved back to the slide she was referring to.

'Yes, the numbers were as per the latest reports that I had got my hands on and I updated it on all the slides.' I had managed to get access to some new data and was happy that I did because the data was recent. It made the projections near accurate and our case very strong. The new data also made the profit margins soar, which was key for securing the investment.

'The data on the last several slides don't correspond and neither does the final figure,' she said slowly, which shook my world.

'What?' I made all the changes myself and I had checked them, or had I? Did I change the data on the last slide? I was not very sure all of a sudden, so I moved to the last slide to check. She was right, I had not made the changes on the last slide. It just needed some calculations and the numbers had to be changed but I was all of a sudden not very sure if I could do it correctly. 'Can you do it?' I asked Adira. She shook her head. Her expertise was client management, and she could handle meetings very well, but when she said that she didn't want to touch the numbers, I understood her apprehensions and didn't pressure her. She pursed her lips and sat thinking. Our screens froze and just like that, it was 2018 again. The same face, the same eyes, her hair falling on her slender neck, her gaze making me want to do everything for her. But it was not 2018 any more, the phones were better, the connection was better, too, so before I could take a screenshot, the phone screen went blank and the device restarted.

Unlike 2018, she was physically very close to me so, instead of making another phone call, she walked up to my room and stood at the door. I quickly grabbed my mask before I growled at her, 'Why do you walk in here when you know that I am contagious?'

She put out her tongue ever so slightly, pressed it between her teeth, and took a few steps back with her hands in the air and all my anger vaporized. She knew her power over me and exactly how and when to use it. I saw her lips stretch into a wide smile and I was at her beck and call already. *Why does the heart not listen to the brain?*

'The call dropped,' she explained. 'So, what are we planning to do now?' she asked.

'I will try and do something. I will ask Piyush or Tamanna to work on it.' Though the couple had been silent partners, they knew everything about the project as I had been sending them weekly updates. It was a small favour to ask, and I knew that they would be more than willing to help, especially because their money was at stake.

'Hmm . . . I would rather hope that you did not disturb them,' Adira said. It occurred to me that I was missing some piece of information there and I waited for her to elaborate. 'Tamanna has caught COVID too. She doesn't have many symptoms, just the loss of smell and a slight fever, but they have a child that Piyush needs to look after and this will be added work.' Under no circumstances was I going to exploit the fact that Piyush and Tamanna were kind people. They had been kind enough to spend on my idea.

'Why did you not tell me?' I asked her, partially knowing the answer.

'You are not well and would have been worried unnecessarily. Tamanna is in a better state than you, but they already have too much on their plates. We need to find another way,' she spoke like a teacher and even though I was feeling like shit, I laughed. She looked at me like I had grown two heads. 'What is so funny?'

'You are, when you try to be all stern and bossy.'

'Ha ha,' she said and pressed her temple with her left finger. 'I think I know someone who is perfect for the job but you might not like him touching your dream project,' she said and I instantly knew who she was talking about.

Go after what you truly want, do not settle.
If you do not want something, just say no; but if you do, do not
wait for it to come to you.

Ronnie

Well, I recall hearing a one-liner in a very popular Hindi movie and that was what was happening in my life at that moment—'Old Villain, Re-entry!'

After not more than fifteen minutes, at seven-thirty, Sid and I were on a video call. I was at his mercy again. I needed his help, and I knew that no amount of ego could help me come out of the situation. I had to keep my ego aside and accept his help graciously. He was being nice by agreeing to help me out and was the bigger person. We awkwardly waited in silence for Adira to join the call. As soon as she joined, he morphed into Mr Charming and I was the donkey from *Shrek*, laughing to cover my lack of charm and showing all my teeth. The call lasted half an hour and Sid fixed the slides for us as I coughed my way through the conversation. He was very good at what he did, and I knew that, if we had met under different circumstances, we could have worked together. But he was interested in Adira and many other girls at the same time and that meant he had to be away from me.

Several times during the call, he mentioned that he was doing the favour only because of Adira and I understood that.

While I did understand him and his favours, my mind plotted ways to kill him but only after he had done my work, that too for free. I coughed a few times and Adira asked me to drop off the call. I did as I was told, mainly because he was done with the corrections on TeachMee's slides and I was not planning to stay there and listen to his lame attempts to woo her again. They were still talking after five minutes and that was when I closed my eyes to give them rest.

It was ten at night when I woke up. My body hurt and my throat ached. I peeped out of the door to find Adira's mother still awake. She turned around to look at me when I coughed. Her spectacles rested on the edge of her nose. I sometimes wonder how and why do parents' spectacles rest at the tip of their noses and everyone else's just rest on the bridge?

'I slept through dinner, I guess,' I said in an attempt to start a conversation.

'You did not, I made khichdi for you,' she told me, getting up and switching off the TV. Within moments, I had a plate full of food and warm water delivered to my door and my growling tummy indicated that I had to eat before I thought of anything or anyone. So I listened to my body and I ate. I was surprisingly hungry, though not much better health-wise. As I ate, her mother parked herself outside; she wanted to talk about something for sure but I had no energy to ask her. I just wanted to finish my food and crawl back into bed. But this woman always got what she wanted and at that moment, she wanted me to give her a ear. So we compromised and I gave her what she wanted; that was the smart thing to do; after all, she was my landlady too.

While I stuffed my face with food, she began telling me how much Adira had changed with my presence in the house and she meant a positive change. I didn't want to interrupt her, but I was indeed very surprised at her statement.

'I mean, she likes not just spending time with you, but you have given her a sense of purpose with this new project of yours. I had lost all hopes of her being so engaged, so involved in anything,' she said, as I continued to eat. I nodded as I did agree with what she was saying. I had seen the changes in her too, but I didn't talk about them out loud as I did not want to jinx anything. No, I am not superstitious as such, but when life throws many things at you that end up hurting you one after the other, every positive thing feels precious to you. This positive change in Adira was precious to me.

Once I was done with my food, I placed my plate outside again to be picked up and went into the washroom in my room to wash my hands. I purposely spent more than the necessary time in there as I was not completely ready to face her mother again. She had started reminding me of my mother and, being so unwell, I needed my family. I didn't want to come across as a weak man, especially not when I was living with two very strong women.

When I finally emerged from the washroom hoping that she had gone to sleep as I really couldn't take any more extreme emotions in my state, I saw her waiting at the door for me. There I was, almost at eleven at night, standing in front of the woman I desperately wanted to be my mother-in-law. She was looking at me with tears ready to roll down her cheeks; she was happy with the developments and so was I. We could have left it at that but no, she wanted to talk to me more about it and probably make me cry too. *Why were the women in my life so adamant about making me show my emotions when all I wanted for them was happiness and laughter?*

Anyway, for obvious reasons, I couldn't ignore her even if I wanted to. So, I did what was expected of me. I walked over to the door ensuring I stayed within the boundaries of the room and sat on the chair. I placed two masks on my face and told her that I, too, had sensed and seen Adira change and I, too, was more than elated with her happiness. She listened to me as I had listened to her, wordlessly, with just a few nods here and there.

She then got up saying, 'I think it is time I forgive you, she wants me to.' *Had they been talking about me? Did Adira ask her mother to make peace with me?* I wondered, taking in the words. I had waited for her to say it for so long. Somewhere in my heart I always knew that Adira and I could never be together until her mother accepted me, until she forgave me for my recklessness in the past, until she wanted me to be a part of her life as a son. I was so overwhelmed with emotion that, had I been well, I would have hugged her only for her to hit me as my mother hits me when I irritate her.

'Thank you . . .' the words escaped my lips and tears fell from my eyes.

'She is happy with you,' she told me and left me with my feelings, standing at the door. I wanted to ask her if Adira was still awake. I had not heard any commotion from around her room since I had woken up. Maybe she had gone to sleep or was probably preparing for the meeting the next day. I was blessed to have her around at that time; she was working tirelessly for my dreams. She knew how important the meeting was for me and she was sacrificing her time, her sleep for me. If this was not love, then I wondered what it was. Thinking of love, thinking of us, I lost myself in the world of dreams. My nightmares were slowly leaving my side and sunny dreams were taking their place.

Love doesn't have to make sense, it has to make one happy, make one feel warm, make one feel complete. Love hurts and yet it is love that heals.

Adira

I had spent a good part of the night before the meeting contemplating, preparing for the next day. Some part of the night was also spent eavesdropping on Mummy and Ronnie. I heard my mother finally accept Ronnie's apology. They had come a long way since the time they'd first met. They cared for each other and I knew that. The trouble was that they didn't know that they cared for each other and over the last several months had even started liking one another like mother and son. Both of them are indispensable in my life and they both know it; they had to get along and finally they did. All it took was an accident and a pandemic for them to realize the obvious. That night, despite all the butterflies in my stomach, I felt at ease and slept soundly.

The next morning at seven I had a meeting with Ronnie's potential investors. He had marked an email to them saying that he would be a part of the meeting but would not be doing the talking as he was down with COVID. I knew how important the project was for him. It could make his career, but what impressed me most was the fact that his idea came from such a noble cause. His heart was in the right place even when he thought of a business and that said a lot about him. If the meeting went well, I had a surprise for him. It was going to change both our lives and I was nervous as well as excited about it.

Sharp at seven, I logged into the call on my laptop. A four-member team from an angel investment company called Sandstorm Investors was on the call already. They had read the email from Ronnie about his health, obviously, and expressed their concern while we all waited patiently for Ronnie to join in. I texted him a few times; however, there was no response from him. So, I asked the board members for permission to go and check if he would be joining in late. 'Sure,' was all a female voice on the other end said before they all muted their audio. I didn't want to screw up the opportunity, but I still pressed mute on the call and dashed towards Ronnie's room. As I passed the kitchen, I found Mummy making chai for herself. 'Is Ronnie up?' I asked her.

'He has not made any noise if he is up, why?' she asked me, confirming my suspicion that he was still sleeping, which was very unlike him. He had not been keeping well and my brain thought of all the things that could have gone wrong. 'Ronnie,' I called out, banging at the door. There was no response. He was a deep sleeper and under normal circumstances, I would have not been worried about him, but I was. I was worried about him and I was worried about his dream project. I knew how much its success mattered to him. I had to manage the situation so, after the third unsuccessful attempt to get him to open the door, I reached out to Mummy again. 'Can you please try and open the door to his room? He is not answering his phone either. I need to get back on the call,' I told her and she switched off the burner and got right to the job.

I shook my head in an attempt to calm myself down and counted till ten. There were people on the call who were waiting for me to return to them. They were big investors and I had to ensure that TeachMee got the funding it needed, single-handedly. I could not let down Ronnie or the others involved in TeachMee. When counting till ten could not calm me down, I practised what Ronnie had once taught me, I closed my eyes and reached my happy place in my mind. My happy place was the Yarra River bridge in Melbourne where Ronnie and I had spent time together to get to know each other better. The calmness of the river and the sun bathing everything around us golden as if it was a dream. Instantly, I got my nerves under control. 'You can do this!' I told myself and closed the door behind me—the sound of my mother calling out Ronnie's name to wake him up ceased in the background. All I could hear and see were the investors in front of me.

The meeting ended in one hour; I was sweating by the end of it. As soon as I pressed the end call button, my mind drifted to Ronnie. My heart beating as if it would jump out of my body, I stepped out of the room and found Mummy still standing at Ronnie's door. The door was still closed. 'Sid is coming with his father, we will break open the door,' Mummy said, pressing her hand into mine. Her palms touched my icy cold hands, making me realize how bad things could be.

Within moments, Sid and his father were over with a few tools. They broke the lock and opened the door. I was the first one to enter the room and found him lying face down on the bed with his face in his pillow. I froze in my spot and allowed my mother to go to his side and shake him. I could not bear the sight.

Every time I was weak, you became my strength.

Adira

Sometimes you think that the person you love is your world and if they leave this world, nothing will be left for you to continue living for. At other times, the same person makes you so angry that you wish you could end their lives with your own two hands. I felt the same when I realized that Ronnie had slept through the most important meeting of his life with music blaring in his ears. What looked like a dead body was his resting body and what nearly gave me a heart attack was him sleeping with Punjabi songs playing on his phone in his ears on loop.

When Mummy shook him, Ronnie leisurely turned to face her and when he noticed that Sid and his father were there too, with tools in their hands, masks and gloves on, he scurried to get up. 'What happened?' he asked everyone and then immediately picked up a mask from his bedside before adding, 'I have corona, you fools!'

'We know that,' Mummy told him with sarcasm dripping in her tone. 'But you are also deaf, I suppose.' She didn't let him respond. Instead, she asked all of us barring Ronnie to step out of the room. Sid and his father went back to their home after tea and Ronnie became the butt of all jokes that afternoon. I thanked both Sid and his father with all my heart before reminding them that they should now get tested if they showed any symptoms. Under normal circumstances, I would have felt very bad for Ronnie because of his illness and the fact that his dream venture was now being handled by others, but not that day. I was furious with him! I had been so worried about him while he slept, unaware of what was happening in the world around him. He didn't talk to me as I went over to his room to scold him after Sid and his father left. He pretended to be asleep when I could see that he was peeping from underneath the blanket. I knew that he was itching to ask about the meeting, but I was not going to tell him. He had to first apologize for being reckless. Maybe he was embarrassed with the turn of events and his foolishness, but he still had to apologize!

In the afternoon, the usual food and chai were delivered to him by Mummy, and she couldn't help but laugh every time she went to his room.

At around nine at night, he opened the door of his room and shouted my name out loud. After lunch, he had been calling and texting me, but I was too angry to respond as none of his initial messages had the word 'sorry' in them. By the evening, I was so upset that I kept my phone in the kitchen and decided to forget about it for the rest of the day.

'Tell me,' I said, standing far from his room with my hands folded across my chest.

'I am sorry,' he said.

'Okay,' was the best I could manage without unleashing my anger on him.

'You never told me what happened at the meeting.' Finally, he wanted to know how it had gone. He had not been there when he should have been, which made me furious. However, he was still unwell and he had been losing weight since COVID had hit him.

'It went okay, I guess,' I told him, intentionally not divulging much information. It was his work; TeachMee was his brainchild so he had to do the work. He had to probe me, he had to ask questions if he needed them answered. After all, I had done him a favour.

'Okay,' he nodded, still not asking me what he wanted to know.

'Anything else?' I asked him upfront. My anger always fizzled as soon as I saw Ronnie and I felt the same happen that evening too. He looked so vulnerable and lost that it was not easy to stay angry with him for long.

'Thank you for taking my place on the call; I am so sorry about the morning,' he finally gave a proper apology and I couldn't help but notice that he sounded a little demotivated. Was he assuming that we didn't get the funding? Probably he was, as a lot was at stake for him.

'Sure, no worries,' I told him and turned on my heel to go back to my room, giggling. Taking a few steps in that direction, I thought of putting him out of misery. 'By the way, they have agreed to fund TeachMee. You have an initial funding of ten million US dollars!'

Before I met you, I didn't have much ambition.
But now, I want to get the moon for you!

Ronnie

'What?' Was I hallucinating? Was this a dream? Or a dream come true? Did she say ten million US dollars!

'You heard me,' she said and vanished into her room. I could see the spring in her step; she was as excited as I was.

I had not looked at my computer since I'd woken up. I was too terrified to check anything online or over email also. I was sure there would have been an email with the minutes of the meeting. Our investors were diligent when it came to putting everything in writing. I didn't check anything because I wanted to know what had happened from her. She had done me a huge favour by replacing me on the call and so I thought it had to come from her.

I sprang on to my bed, immediately fired up my computer and logged in to check my emails. There it was! An email confirming exactly what Adira had said. We had bagged our first-ever funding and TeachMee was finally going to start, develop and expand. My dream venture finally had the wings that it needed to soar high in the sky! Not caring about my high fever, I shot messages to Tamanna and Piyush and forwarded them the email too. After all, the seed money belonged to the three of us and we were equal partners. I even asked them if we could include Adira on board as an equal partner for all her efforts and work.

As soon as the email went out of my mailbox, I got a call from a very elated Piyush. He was happy with Adira's inclusion and so was his wife. I checked upon Tamanna's health. She was COVID negative as of that day and Baby Adira was finally in her mother's lap. I sent in a message to Adira too to let her know of her being on board. As expected, she was over the moon. She already had more than a million ideas for the app. The next several hours went in phone calls. I called my parents, spoke to my sister and her husband who were initially not very convinced with the idea but now were proud of me for going ahead with it anyway.

Outside my room, I could hear Adira talking to her mother chirpily and telling her that she was back to work as a director. I could feel her happiness seep into me and make me a tad better. Thankfully, everyone forgave me for sleeping through such an important meeting; after all, I was still unwell.

Later that night, I pinged Adira:

Me: THANK YOU

Adira: FOR WHAT?

Me: FOR BELIEVING IN ME & TEACHMEE

Adira: YOU ARE WELCOME

Me: AND FOR TAKING THE CALL TODAY FOR ME

Adira: I AM ONE OF THE DIRECTORS. WHY WOULD I HAVE NOT TAKEN THE CALL?

Me: :-)

Adira: YOU HAVE ANOTHER COVID TEST TOMORROW

Me: I HOPE I COME OUT NEGATIVE. I AM FEELING MUCH BETTER ANYWAY

Adira: You are feeling better because I got you Ten Million Dollars

Me: Yes, that too

Some more of our mindless banter continued through the night. While we made some silly plans to celebrate once I was COVID-free, I knew that I had some serious planning to do. I also had to plan the most enchanting surprise for her.

Sometimes it goes very quiet in my heart, so quiet that all I hear is your name.

Ronnie

A week later…

All the fireworks around TeachMee had died down finally and we were back to business. It was the middle of July and we were anticipating monsoon rains any time. There was a lot of work. I had resigned from my regular nine-to-five job and so had Piyush. Tamanna had taken a maternity break, so she was yet to take over her role. The app needed an upgrade and the bandwidth to be able to be launched pan India. One might think that ten million dollars is a lot of money but when it gets to launching something pan India, hiring a team, and bearing the costs of initial videos that were world-class, the money was not that much. We had to go bigger and we knew that soon, we had to make it profitable. While all of this was happening, I had a very important task at hand.

Meanwhile, I had fully recovered from COVID and had tested negative twice. So, my morning teas were now sipped in the presence of Adira and her mother. While her mother had already permitted me to be with Adira, I was yet to ask Adira if she wanted to be with me again.

After tea, I went into my room and opened a red jewellery box. Inside it was a gold ring, a simple gold band, without a precious stone. I knew that Adira deserved the best, but I was no rich man when I bought the ring with the Rs 15,000 savings I had. I was a nine-to-five employee who had limited means. I did indeed want to give her everything that she needed and deserved and more, but for this occasion, I believed that the simple gold ring was what I should go for. The ring was a replica of her great-grandmother's ring. She had once shown me a photo and I had taken a picture of the grainy photo with my phone. She believed that her great-grandfather and great-grandmother had a beautiful love story, something that could inspire generations to come. Her great-grandfather loved his wife to the core, and I had similar feelings for Adira. I had my mother's trusted jeweller make the ring on order and had it since before the accident. I had hidden it under her pillow on the night of the fateful accident and never really got a chance to give it to her. And since then, I had just been waiting.

I know waiting for the pandemic to be over would have been the wise choice, but I have waited enough for things to be perfect. Sometimes it is not what is happening around us that matters; it is what is happening within us that matters the most. I wanted to make Adira mine forever and there was no right time or place to pop the question. I just had to have the right intent, which I did.

So, I discussed my plans with Adira's mother, who was thrilled with the news. Had the last few weeks not happened, I would have lost my balance at her reaction, but now I knew that she liked me enough to keep me around.

'What do you have in mind?' she asked me.

We can't do anything fancy, but I was hoping to order in her favourite pizza from Domino's, a quiet afternoon with you gone and a proposal,' I told her, emphasizing the word 'gone'.

'We can't do that, I have nowhere to go,' she told me to my face. With COVID spreading, she hardly had a place to go to without the fear of getting infected. Under no circumstances could I ask her to risk her life just because I wished to propose to her daughter. Nodding in understanding, I absent-mindedly ran my fingers through my hair. 'We can do this on the terrace,' I suggested.

'It is very hot on the terrace during the mornings. Adira doesn't even want to go there for her morning exercises.' She had raised a valid point.

'It is a very hot and humid day, indeed. We can set up a few fans there in the evening and instead of lunch pizza we can do a dinner pizza,' I suggested a more rational plan and her mother nodded in agreement this time.

So, it was decided—I wanted the dinner to be a surprise so I quietly placed two pedestal fans on the terrace while she took a shower.

Once the mat and a few cushions were moved, time started passing very slowly. I had never been this nervous in my entire life. People think that proposals are important in a girl's life but they never really talk about how nerve-racking it is for a man to ask the girl he loves if she would like to spend her life with him. *What if she says no?* I wondered. *If she says no, I will respect that,* I told myself. She had the right to reject me like I had the right to feel rejected.

All through the day, she kept talking about TeachMee, the way she thought we could strategize social media marketing, etc. She had a few companies in mind that we could outsource the work to, but my brain cells were drunk on the idea of spending my life with her. So all I did was look at her like a love-struck puppy.

'Are you even listening to me?' she asked me, upset over something. *Was I listening to her?* Not really, I was looking at how her earrings moved as she spoke, how the sunlight bounced off her skin and how she moved her hair away from her face. I was enchanted.

'Sorry, I was thinking of something else.' I had to be honest because I had no idea what she was trying to explain to me.

'Something else? What is more important at this time than this?' She was angry and looked at me, squinting her eyes. I wondered if I had ever told her how cute she looked when she was angry; her cheeks flushed and her nose crinkled a bit.

'You,' I said, resting my chin in my palm and looking at her closely.

Her cheeks grew pinker, and this time not because of anger. She looked down at the notebook she had and her lush hair fell all over it and her face, covering my view. While I contemplated if it was okay to take a few strands away from her face and look her in the eye, someone stomped into the study. Of course, it was my future mother-in-law! Or at least I hoped that she would be my mother-in-law soon.

She was there to announce lunch. Both of us followed her into the dining area quietly and parked ourselves at the table. Normally, I helped her cook and clean but Adira's mother had insisted that I did not follow her into the kitchen that afternoon. I was surprised to see bhindi for lunch. It looked just like the one my mother made for me during summers, crunchy and spicy. Adira's mother was making an effort, so I remembered to compliment her as soon as I took the first bite. The rest of the lunch was spent in silence with a few questions around general things bouncing across the table. It was mainly the mother and daughter talking to each other as I was busy taming the butterflies in the pit of my stomach.

Immediately after lunch, I retired to my room to call my parents. My mother was thrilled at the prospect of me proposing and my father was happy that I was finally doing the right thing.

'We have managed to get two tickets on a repatriation flight to India,' my mother informed me, clapping her hands in happiness. 'I want to be there for the wedding,' she said and I had to remind her that Adira had not said yes, yet. 'That is because you have not asked her yet! She loves you and will be very happy with you.' Talk about Indian mothers and their blind love for their sons. I wanted to tell her that Adira deserved better but I was in no mood to argue so I changed the topic to my sister and her kids. They were all well and the call ended soon because one of her children decided to cry at the top of their lungs.

'Okay bye, beta, keep us informed. Our flight is on the first of August so do not plan anything before we come back!' She could be the brand ambassador of positive thinking. I had so much more pressure now—what would I tell them if things went south? I wondered, trying to find a playlist on Amazon Prime Music for the evening. I wanted things to be as beautiful as possible under the present circumstances. I also tried to get some flowers but that was a fail. No florist would deliver so I decided to sacrifice a few flowers from Adira's mother's terrace garden. She had a few different kinds of roses and a few hibiscuses that had to do the job.

Next on my list was a peppy paneer pizza from Domino's. It had to be cheese burst like they show in their commercial. So, I rang the nearest Domino's and asked to speak to the manager. 'I am proposing and your pizza is very important for me,' I told Neeru, the manager. She was happy to help out and took my order of two large pizzas to be delivered sharp at seven. It was six-thirty by the time I was done with all the preparations upstairs. Every time I went up and down the stairs Adira eyed me suspiciously and I wondered whether her mother had stabbed me in back and revealed my secret.

There was little I could do, so I took a quick shower, dressed in a plain white shirt and denims, and put the ring in my pocket. The plan was to present the ring after we ate the pizza. I knocked on her door and she walked out dressed in a lilac salwar kameez, her hair loose and the bracelet was the only accessory that I had eyes for.

'You look stunning,' I told her the moment I regained my speech.

'Thank you,' she said promptly. 'So where are you taking me?' she asked, draining the colour from my face. She knew! I looked around to see her mother who just shrugged as if telling me that it was all my fault that the surprise was ruined.

'Do not look at her like that. She told me only when I pestered her enough!' Adira said.

'Is that so?' escaped my mouth as I threw daggers with my gaze towards her mother.

'Yes,' Adira said and intertwined her hands in mine. 'Mummy said that you are planning a dinner with just you and me, so where are we going?' she asked, breaking the trance I was sliding into since she had touched me.

'Just to the terrace as there is no other place safe enough nowadays. But we need to wait for the dinner before we go upstairs.' And just then, as if on cue, the doorbell rang. It was the guy from Domino's. He had our order and I peeped in to make sure the pizza was, in reality, bursting with cheese, which it was. I kept a pizza and a bottle of Coke on the kitchen counter for her mother and gave her a smile which she returned. My luck that evening was great.

Thanking my stars for making things work as per plan for once in my life, I signalled Adira to lead the way towards the terrace. Holding the railing with one hand and taking my hand with the other, she walked ahead of me. On our way up, I turned once to find her mother looking for the TV remote. She had no intention of eavesdropping and that gave me one less thing to worry about.

When we reached the terrace, the sun was setting, casting an orange hue everywhere. I had set up a mat and a few cushions in the centre. Two fans buzzed in the background. Thankfully, the air had become misty and pleasant, too. Three sets of fairy lights lit the area around the mat making it look romantic. Those were Adira's words, not mine. She loved the set-up and gazed at it with childlike enthusiasm as she moved forward with steady steps while I followed her with food in my hands and hope in my heart.

We had a delightful dinner with conversations mostly around the venture and her plans for marketing it. I realized there that she was my soulmate; she was so passionate about things that I cared for that it excited me. She brought calm to my otherwise turbulent life. I also understood that evening what a soulmate should feel like in your life; they do not always bring fluttering heartbeats and crazy passion. These things come and go in a relationship, but a soulmate brings in calm and peace. They make your heart warm with love.

By the time we polished off the pizza, it was nearly eight at night. The sun had long set, and the moonlight was dim. The fairy lights enabled us to see each other's faces. The heat of the day had also gone completely and now the air was scented as if it had rained somewhere nearby. Under normal circumstances, a cool breeze and a full stomach are enough for me to sleep like a baby, but that evening I didn't even want to blink for I didn't want to miss even a single expression that came and went by on her face.

'That was fun!' she said and looked up at the sky. Her eyes were wide and sparkling, her hair now behind her ears away from her face. It was the perfect moment to propose. I fiddled in my pockets and found the ring. Holding it tightly in my palm, I let out a deep breath. *You can do this*! I told myself and that was the moment when she shifted her focus back to me. Her eyes sparkled as she bit her lower lip innocently as if anticipating something

'I . . . I mean . . .' I was out of words again. *Why does this always happen to me?* I wondered as and she raised her left eyebrow in a very quirky way. I was nervous and her actions were not making it any better for me.

I sighed again to focus on the task at hand. I needed some distance between us to be able to talk so I stood up with a jerk and instantly regretted the decision. After sitting on the pillows, my knees didn't like the sudden jerk and jump. I had no time to ponder over it or let the pain take me down, so I ignored my aching left knee. I decided to go down on my good right knee. She knew what was happening and I saw tears build up in the corners of her eyes. *Was she happy or sad?* I didn't know because she had shielded her face with her palms as soon as she saw me looking deep into her eyes. I had to start what I finished but I still waited for her to compose her emotions. She blinked a few times and that was it.

You might ask what that was. Well, that was the moment the skies opened up and fat drops started falling one after the other on us, drenching us and spoiling my proposal. I helped her get up and leaving the mat and the cushions where they were, we took shelter in the gazebo, with winds blowing rain everywhere. There was hardly any space for both of us to be safe from rain and my rational mind suggested that I do the right thing. The right thing was to take her downstairs, away from the rain. The proposal had to wait.

*Every time a plan fails, every time you face a rejection, remember
that something greater is on its way.*

Ronnie

Sometimes, everything happens for a reason that is meant to lead you to what is meant for you. As we walked downstairs, I saw red and silver balloons scattered on the stairs on our way down. I looked at Adira quizzically and she just shrugged; she didn't know what was happening either. As unbelievable as it sounded, it was quite likely that her mother had decided to celebrate the proposal. What made it awkward was the fact that the said celebrated proposal had not yet taken place. Some days I am glad that my parents are not as involved in my life as Adira's mother is in hers; that was one of those days. The woman was determined to make me look like a fool and spoil what I had planned to be the most memorable moment of my life.

Pushing through the balloons, we managed to reach the living room. Her mother was nowhere to be seen. The best course of action was to now get down on my knee again and propose to her before her mother paraded back into the living room. But Adira beat me to it. The moment I turned to face her, my jaw dropped. Adira stood with her hand stretched out and a golden band in her palm. 'You remember I told you about my great-grandfather?' she asked and I just nodded. 'This is the ring that my badi dadi gave to him. He wore it every day of his life. I believe that no man can be a better husband, father, or friend than him. I want what my great-grandparents had and I want that with you because even though we have made mistakes in this relationship, our love is greater and more powerful than all of them,' she said in one breath and exhaled. I didn't have any words to add; she had said it all and she had done that better than I would have. I just fished out the ring. 'We think alike and we plan alike too,' I said. 'I had planned to propose to you with this ring, hoping that you would say "yes".'

Laughing and crying simultaneously, we exchanged rings in the presence of her mother, who, by the way, had been listening to everything from the kitchen like a sly cat. She had been the one who had blown up all the balloons and planned it with Adira while she also planned my version of the proposal. I was glad that her mother was on my side now as, under no circumstances, did I want to be on the hit list of a woman who makes plans in such cunning ways and ensures that she meets her goals one way or the other. As we hugged, I felt calmness bathe me.

It is important to learn how to forgive. She forgave me because she has a big heart. It is also imperative that we learn to forgive ourselves. Most times we are ruthless with ourselves. We must learn to be kind when we look back at our actions and let things go.

Mistakes are a part of us, but they are not everything that we are made up of.
Past mistakes should not define and dictate everything for the rest of our lives.

Present

On the 3rd of May 2021, Adira and Ronnie got married at Ronnie's house in Delhi. Adira wore her mother's wedding saree and her teary-eyed mother gave her daughter away and did her kanyadaan. Ronnie's immediate family managed to fly down and Tamanna, Piyush, and Baby Adira were present too. It was a small Hindu ceremony followed by lunch. Not every love story needs a lot of noise around it. The highlight of the wedding was the ring-bearer, Samba. He followed guests around, stopping for snack breaks and pats and then passed out next to the couple as they sat for the pheras next to the holy havan kund.

Adira's leg remains a reminder of the accident but her heart has moved on. Ronnie's start-up has gained a lot of coverage in the tech market and all the directors are happy to contribute their working hours towards making it a bigger brand. As I write this last note, Ronnie and Adira are expecting their first child and are in America for a client meeting. The couple plans to shuttle between India and America as they expand their business horizons. Ronnie's parents now fly to three continents and are enjoying their lives. Samba, being too old to travel, remains stationed at Adira's mother's house.